IN-LAWFUL
HOMICIDE

IN-LAWFUL HOMICIDE

MOTHER OF ALL
MURDER MYSTERIES

BRADLIE K. ROBERTS

251 CF

IN-LAWFUL HOMICIDE
Written by Bradlie K. Roberts
Copyright © 2023 by Bradlie K. Roberts
ALL RIGHTS RESERVED

Cover Design by Studio 251

Originally published June 26, 2023, under the title:
"Murder at Magnolia Castle" (978-0-9822775-8-4)

ISBN (eBook): 979-8-9906096-6-2
ISBN (Paperback): 979-8-9936709-0-4

251 CRIME FICTION
P.O. Box 551
Gloucester, MA 01931

This book is dedicated to
everyone who enjoys cozying up
with a good book, like me!

TABLE OF CONTENTS

MAGNOLIA CASTLE

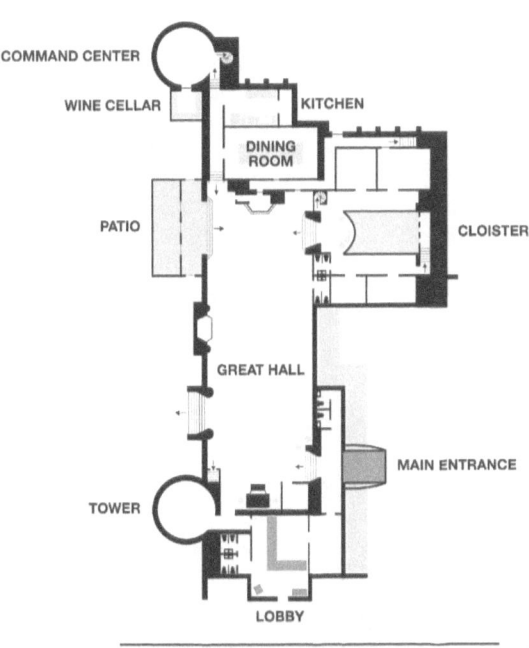

COMMAND CENTER

WINE CELLAR

KITCHEN

DINING ROOM

PATIO

CLOISTER

GREAT HALL

MAIN ENTRANCE

TOWER

LOBBY

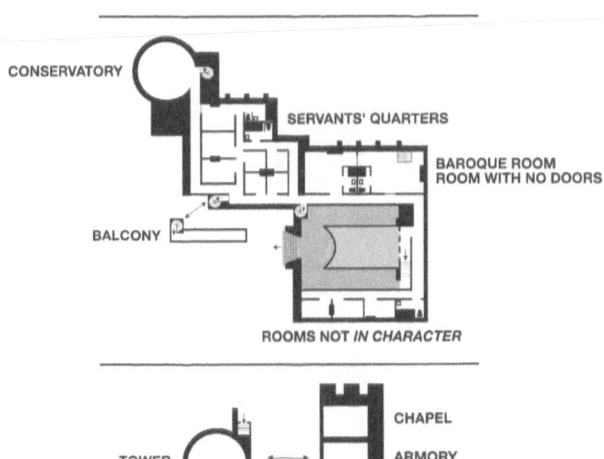

CONSERVATORY

SERVANTS' QUARTERS

BAROQUE ROOM
ROOM WITH NO DOORS

BALCONY

ROOMS NOT *IN CHARACTER*

TOWER

CHAPEL

ARMORY

DUNGEON

Prologue

NEWS FLASH:
MURDER AT MAGNOLIA CASTLE!

"This is Jeff Jamison bringing you a breaking story from WPZ News. The coastal town of Popplestone, Massachusetts, —known for its sandy beaches and old-world charm—was rocked overnight by news of a grisly murder at famed Magnolia Castle.

"Renowned for its stunning blend of Gothic and Renaissance European architectural styles, the castle has held a prominent place in the annals of modern history, welcoming world leaders and hosting lavish weddings. It has also become a cherished venue for local residents, who fondly associate it with lively musical concerts and the vibrant Popplestone Renaissance Festival, an annual tradition that draws crowds from far and wide.

"Now, in the aftermath of one of the season's most violent storms, first responders are swarming the grounds, not because of the tempest outside but one inside its hallowed walls. I have to say, it's an eerie sight, watching emergency vehicles' lights flash against the castle's noble stone facade—especially with everything cordoned off with bright yellow tape. And look, a steady stream of early morning strollers and dog walkers are being turned away, visibly shaken by the chaotic scene.

"Wait. This just in: our very own Karen Eagan is hovering over the castle grounds in WPZ Chopper 1 with exclusive information about this tragic event. Take it away, Karen."

"Thanks, Jeff. I'm here, where mere hours ago, two of the area's most well-known families gathered for a wedding, but this event was much more than just a ceremony; it was a celebration of a lifelong love story between Marco Amato, state-champion quarterback of Popplestone's Longliner's football team, and Toni Bellagamba, a budding artist and advocate for local charities, including her successful *Pies for Paws* campaign held during Popplestone Days on Main Street each year.

"By all accounts, the atmosphere inside the castle was filled with laughter and anticipation as loved ones gathered in one of the East Coast's most picturesque settings. However, what should have been a joyous occasion took a terrible turn, shifting from celebration to confusion and heartbreak. The families who had come together to celebrate love have now found themselves united in sorrow.

"I think I see something…yes…Rick, can you zoom in? Right there! Look! Three people are being led to police cars. And over there, the paramedics are loading someone into an ambulance.

"As our viewers at home just witnessed, an individual is currently being transported to Popplestone Hospital. We don't have any information regarding their medical status or condition, but I'm hearing local authorities are expected to hold a news conference later today to provide updates on this ongoing situation. This is Karen Eagan reporting live for WPZ News, dedicated to bringing you all the latest updates as they unfold. Back to you, Jeff."

1. How It Began

"Oh my Gawd, the two-timing witch came," Francesca Bellagamba-Amato said as she knit-one-purl-two'd her way along needles she'd picked up at the Popplestone Sea Fair. The coarse wool she used was so scratchy it would have made an excellent torture device, but she didn't care. It got cold at night, and she had every intention of making sure her hat was up to the job. Otherwise, why bother knitting it?

Living on New England's rocky coastline hardened a person like no other place, and although her hair had retained its beautiful black sheen (helped by a stock of dye she kept in a cabinet underneath the sink), it had long since thinned. Consequently, hats were a constant accessory to her typically weather-beaten attire. Today, however, she wasn't wearing a hat, at least, not what she'd call a hat. The useless frilly thing perched on her head wasn't good for anything other than getting in the way of seeing people arrive for her son Marco's wedding.

"Who came, Frankie?" Valentina Bellagamba asked, reaching around her voluminous breasts and ample belly to haul up her hose. Val's hair was still black, naturally, which grated on her older sister's nerves.

"Val! Take the cotton out of your ears. I said Rose is here!"

"What? I thought she was dead," the middle Bellagamba sister exclaimed, struggling to pull out the pieces of cotton she'd stuck deep into her ears. She might have had no choice but to remain close to her sister, but she didn't have to listen to her!

"Rose does seem worthy of smiting," Frankie said, peering over her half-completed hat, "but no luck yet. Then again, if the good Lord doesn't do it, I'm sure there are plenty of other people who'd be willing to take up the mantle. Look at her. Who does she think she is, wearing a dress like that at her age? Put on a frickin' bra, ya hussie!"

Val craned her neck to see out of the castle lobby's weather-beaten window. Technically, it was the museum's gift shop, but Frankie had insisted that a couple of chairs and a sofa be brought in for them. "I wish mine were still that perky. Oh, sorry, Father," she said, making the sign of the cross. Well, most of it. Being round and lumpy made it hard to do the whole thing without making an obscene gesture, so Val had adapted it. She certainly didn't want to offend her Savior.

Frankie let out a sound that was somewhere between a cough and a laugh. "Who are you kidding? Yours were never perky."

Val turned back around in a huff. It was true, she'd always been the most well-endowed Bellagamba sister, but Frankie had a way of making even that sound like a bad thing.

The truth was, Val didn't enjoy spending time with her older sister, but she was glad Frankie had insisted they install themselves near the castle's entrance. This way, the mothers of the bride and groom could see—and comment—on everyone as they arrived for the ceremony. It was the most fun she'd had in years.

Outside, the youngest Bellagamba sister made an unsubtle show of her leg as she adjusted the straps on her shoe. The golden rays of the early morning sun made it look like she'd stepped out of a movie. This was not lost on the limousine driver, who paused to admire the view before rounding the car to open the trunk.

"Yoo-hoo!" Rosamunda Gabriella Angelina Bellagamba Trevisani cooed, sounding remarkably like a pigeon with a head cold as she shuffled across the parking lot. In case no one noticed her skin-tight bodycon red dress, flowing ginger hair, and flower-covered hat, she waved an equally floral silk neck scarf over her head as she approached the museum shop's door.

Inside, Frankie made a point of getting the desk attendant's attention. "Brace yourself. She's a handful."

The professional-looking woman on the other side of the counter raised her head disdainfully and nodded, acknowledging the warning.

"I think it's nice that Rose came," Val said, doing a poor job of straightening the wrinkles in her godet gown.

Frankie laugh-coughed again. "Mark my words, she ain't nothing but trouble."

Val didn't say anything because, one, there was no point in arguing with her older sister, and two, Frankie was right.

• • • • •

"Aren't you a strapping young man?" Rose said to a ruggedly handsome gentleman leaning against the bell tower.

He held a smoldering cigarette nonchalantly in one hand and smoothed his slicked-back, red hair with the other. His pinstriped suit did a poor job of hiding his broad shoulders and bulging muscles, the kind of muscles that knew a hard day's work.

Rose flicked her scarf in the man's direction. "Be a good boy and bring those to my room, would you?"

"But I'm not the—"

"Now, don't make a fuss. Run along."

The man shrugged, ripped off the end of his smoke, and put the unfinished part into his breast pocket. The getup was a rental that he didn't have to pay for, so what did he care?

"I'm on the clock," the limo driver said as he removed a cornucopia of bags, boxes, and suitcases from the trunk.

"What of it?" the pin-striped man asked, sauntering over.

"The longer I hang about, the more I cost."

This revelation didn't appear to have any impact. "No skin off my nose."

"You a groomsman?" the driver asked, holding out a box that was held together with a wide, red bow.

"*The* groomsman, you could say."

"Ah. The best man."

"Exactly. Name's Edoardo Bernardi, but everyone calls me Eddo."

The driver thought about this for a moment before saying, "I knew a Bernardi once. Joe Bernardi. Captain of the *K.T. Ann*. A lobster boat, I think."

"That's the one. He's my dad."

"Small world."

"Isn't it, though?" Eddo said, gathering Rose's luggage into his arms.

"Say, what are you doin' playing bellboy?" the driver asked. "The best man's usually got stuff to do."

Eddo shrugged again and disappeared through the castle's side entrance.

2. A Rose By Any Other Name

"Well, well, well. Look what the cat dragged in," Frankie said as Rose tripped through the entrance, caught herself an instant before disaster struck, and casually straightened her dress.

Val giggled.

Frankie didn't miss a beat. "Nice shoes. If those heels were any taller, you'd hit your head on the ceiling. Hey, that's a good idea. Maybe it would knock some sense into you."

"Hey, Rosie. You look nice," Val said, stifling more giggles.

Rose smiled in Val's direction, pointedly not acknowledging her eldest sister.

"We weren't sure you'd come."

"Come?" Frankie asked. "Your overripe sister here thought you were dead."

Val blushed. "Honest mistake. We haven't seen you in a long time."

"I've been abroad."

Frankie's thin lips curled into a wicked smile. "Rose, you've been a broad since you were seventeen."

Val slapped her hand over her mouth, trying not to laugh out loud.

Rose harumphed, turned with exaggerated flair, and shuffled over to the front desk.

As she did this, Eddo appeared with her luggage, dropped it in a pile near an old magazine stand that held whale-watching brochures and the typical assortment of memoirs, histories, and fantasy tales by local authors. Next to it was a large sign that read *Swordstrike! Watch fishermen battle the elements...and each other...in the treacherous North Atlantic.*

"What? Are you planning to stay the year?" Frankie asked. "You know it's only one night, right?"

Rose didn't answer.

"May I help you?" the attendant asked, flashing a poor excuse for a smile. She was wearing a tailored suit that was impeccably pressed. The only thing out of place was a lock of hair, brought on by Francesca Bellagamba-related stress. By the end of the day, the weary attendant expected to be bald, drunk, or both. Then again, events were the bread and butter of the castle, so she did her best to keep up the act.

Rose squinted her eyes as she read the helpful woman's name tag. "Grrr-etta. Gretta, with two t's. How quaint. And five gold stars. I suppose that means something."

"It does. Would you care for a chocolate?" Gretta held out a half-filled bowl of individually wrapped treats from Michol's Candies as Rose fumbled with her wristlet. It was the least a five-star employee of the *Cape Eider Hospitality Group Ltd.* could do for a paying customer—the very least.

When it became apparent that Rose wasn't going to take a candy, Gretta slid the bowl behind the register. She had to keep it hidden, or the help took them by the handful, which wouldn't have been an issue if old Michol didn't think so highly of his confectionery concoctions.

"Aren't you the sweetest thing?" Rose asked, pulling out a gold business card. She slid it over to the attendant as if this conveyed some unspoken level of importance.

It didn't, but Gretta played along. "What a lovely design," the attendant said, reading the name imprinted on the card in frilly gold letters. "Welcome to Magnolia Castle, Mrs.—"

Rose cut her off before she finished. "I bet this place has lots of secrets."

"If you're inquiring about what we offer here at CEHG's premier wedding destination, I can offer you a complimentary map."

Gretta reached over to Rose's side of the counter and retrieved a trifold brochure from the plastic stand. It had a picture of the castle's iconic drawbridge and main entrance on the front, surrounded by towering rhododendrons in full bloom. Flanked by the enormous bushes, a bride and groom smiled as a photographer took their picture.

"Mmhmm," the youngest Bellagamba sister said, pretending to care. Rose didn't do maps.

Gretta placed it on the counter and asked, "Are you with the wedding party?"

"No, but I *am* staying here. It's a perk of being an aunt, I suppose. I made a reservation under the name Trevisani. T-r-e..." she whispered as if it were a secret.

"No need to spell it. It's a common enough name on the Cape, and it's on your card," Gretta said, handing Rose a packet of papers. "If you'd please sign here and here...and here."

"Here you said?"

"No, there."

"Ah, silly me."

"Yeah, you're a laugh riot," Frankie mumbled as she finished a row and kept knitting.

"Don't mind her," Rose said, struggling with the pen. "My sister stubbed her toe when God handed out personalities. By the time she stood up, he'd passed her by."

Val tried to get Frankie's attention, but her older sister pretended not to see her flailing arms.

"Let me help you," Gretta said, taking the pen from Rose and depressing the top. "All you have to do is push the button."

"Oh, how clever!"

Frankie sighed loudly from the sofa.

While Rose signed, Gretta pulled out a broad-tipped pen, opened the brochure she'd left on the counter, and circled several areas. "This afternoon and evening's festivities will be taking place throughout the castle and grounds. Here, we have a scenic overlook for photographs from which you can see Jonah's Reef, Sandy Bar Lighthouse, and the breakwater through the arches. And here, on the western part of the grounds, is the cemetery and wishing well—"

"I always thought that was an odd combination," Rose said, cutting her off. "Who wants to make a wish surrounded by dead people?"

"Ah-hem," Frankie's hoarse voice interrupted again, sounding scratchier than her wool.

"Oh yes. That's where Jimi proposed to you," Rose said. Then she turned to Gretta and repeated herself. "That's where Jimi, Frankie's husband, proposed to her."

"She heard you the first time, Rose. She's standing three feet from you. And she knows Jimi. Who do you think paid for all of this?"

"I was being polite."

"At least you got *your* wish," Val said under her breath. "Some of us have thrown a lot of coins into that well and still aren't married."

Ignoring the bickering sisters, Gretta plowed ahead, determined to finish her spiel. "Be sure to make a wish for the happy couple. Coins tossed into the well today will be donated to Ruff Day Rescue."

"Isn't that nice, Frankie?" Rose asked, addressing her sister directly. "You could wish for some manners."

Frankie paused her knitting long enough to say, "Ha ha," and returned to her purls.

"I think supporting the local animal shelter's a wonderful idea," Val said. "Everyone has a rough day now and then. I've already made several wishes."

"Was one of them for hose that don't run?" Frankie asked.

Val gathered her dress around her waist so she could see, and true enough, two ladders stretched from her ankles to her knees. "I don't know. I just don't know," she grunted, pushing herself out of the chair and rushing out of the room. "I'm glad I brought extras."

Rose turned back around. "Do go on."

Gretta pointed to the map on the inside of the brochure. "Here's where the wedding party will enter the castle."

"Can't I go through there?" Rose asked, pointing behind the desk to a passageway she knew led to the building's great hall.

"This area isn't open to the public. It's reserved for employees at all times of the day," the attendant explained, her pleasant expression more strained than before. "Also, the bride and groom—"

"Ah-hem!" Frankie cleared her throat again.

Correcting herself, Gretta said, "The groom's mother has asked that the wedding party make a grand entrance over the drawbridge, where they will be photographed before the evening's festivities. At that time, the guests will be asked to leave their electronic devices at the door."

"What?" Rose asked, dropping her bag and leaving it dangling listlessly from her wrist.

Frankie smiled with fake kindness. "That's right, sister dearest. A whole night without your precious social media. Whatever will you do?"

"But what if something goes wrong and someone needs help?" Rose asked, obviously flustered.

"Our escape room packages are board-certified and perfectly safe," Gretta said, handing the brochure to Rose. "Additionally, patrons are provided with an emergency button for immediate extraction."

"Whew. You had me going there for a minute. Where is it?"

"What?" Gretta asked, activating Rose's key.

"The button. Where is it?"

"My apologies, but knowledge of its location is restricted to one participant. We find that if too many people know where it is, they tend not to take the experience seriously."

Trying to sound as endearing as possible, Rose said, "You can tell me, honey. I won't say a word."

"That'd be a first," Frankie mumbled, pulling out more yarn.

Gretta looked at her with absolutely no hint of an expression on her face. "You'll have to speak with the event coordinator."

"Great. Who's that?" Rose asked.

"Mrs. Bellagamba-Amato."

Frankie stopped knitting, looked at her youngest sister, and smiled.

To hide her frustration, Rose pretended to look for something in her bag.

"That's right, sis. And you know what? I don't have a clue where it is. Only Father does."

"Who's father?"

"Not someone's father, you daft woman, *the* Father. Father Abraham. He's officiating the service and staying with us for the night if the game lasts that long."

Rose lost it. "Are you kidding? That bastard?"

"Now, now. Watch your language, little Rosie."

"I'll say a few Hail Marys later."

"I'm quite sure you have much more to atone for than swearing at a priest. And don't speak about your brother that way."

"Brother-in-Law, thank you very much!" Rose snapped.

"He's still family. Besides, Jimi wanted him to officiate, so that's that. You can take it up with him if you'd like, but I doubt it would make a difference. Jimi's put in so many years as harbormaster in this town that he's become impervious to changing his mind. I should know."

"Yeah, I can't imagine you and your hubby arguing. It'd be like two mountains telling each other to move."

"We have our moments."

"I bet you do. Anyway, are you sure you can't tell me?" Rose pleaded with Gretta.

"I'm sorry. It's not my place," the attendant explained.

"Fudge nuggets!"

Frankie chuckled and returned to her knitting.

Losing some of her charm, Rose rounded on Gretta. "I'll have you know that I came here as a girl. I know this place's ins and outs better than anyone. Even the places you've taken off exhibit, like the secret wine cellar. I doubt this button-thingy will be too hard to find."

Gretta smiled wanly. "Actually, the wine cellar is currently available for viewing. It houses several fine vintages and is accessed…" She paused to take the map back from Rose and point to its location. "…here, through a secret door in the Command Center. All you have to do is follow the map."

"Yes, yes. I just said I know how to get there."

"Mother caught her making out with the Vanzetti boy in there when she was—"

"We were playing hide-and-seek, thank you very much!"

"Did he find everything you wanted him to find?" Frankie asked.

"I wish you'd—"

Gretta deftly inserted herself in the argument. "I meant no offense. Some people find navigating the castle challenging. Especially the circular stairs."

Frankie sat up in the seat. "Don't worry. Rose is many things, but *challenging* ain't one of 'em."

"And what's that supposed to mean?" Rose asked, her voice rising in volume and pitch.

"How many is it now? Three? Four?"

"Five if you must know, but who's counting."

"You go through men like water through a scupper."

"At least they aren't related," Rose said, knowing she was about to strike a nerve. "Nothing better than a little inbreed-ing to keep things in the family."

"You little—"

"I only speak the truth."

In a flash, Frankie was standing in front of Rose, having launched herself out of the chair with such force that Gretta flinched.

Brandishing her knitting needles in an exceedingly threat-ening way, she yelled, "You know Toni and Marco aren't blood relations. Val did a good thing by taking her in. That kid's been through the wringer. We should all be so lucky."

Rose didn't move. She didn't even breathe, and the room got eerily quiet.

The fact that Val and Frankie Bellagamba's children had fallen in love was more than a bit of a sore spot in the family. It didn't matter that Val had adopted Toni following a tragic boating accident that took the lives of her first adoptive parents. Toni and Marco were technically cousins, which felt odd to just about everyone except them.

Rose shifted her weight between her feet. "I—"

There was a crash as Eddo tossed the last load of Rose's luggage into the room, and the tension of the moment broke.

Looking defeated, Frankie went back to her spot on the sofa. "It might be a moot point, anyway."

Also softening, Rose asked, "What do you mean?"

"They want to call it off."

"The wedding? Why?"

"They had a big argument."

"About what?"

"No idea. Val and I locked them in that room upstairs. You know, the one with no way out."

"Sure, the Wallpaper Room."

"That's the one. We figured they needed a little alone time to sort through things, but it isn't going well by the sound of it."

For the first time, Rose noticed the hint of muffled yelling echoing between the castle's stone walls. "Sorry, Frankie. I didn't know."

"How could you? You're never around."

Rose didn't take the bait. She was the only Bellagamba to have left the island, and she had no intention of apologizing. People who lived on the Cape loathed to cross the bridge to the mainland, and most of the time, they didn't need to. Popplestone had all the amenities of a big city without the fuss, not to mention a wide variety of sandy, rocky, or pebbly beaches to choose from, direct access to the water, and a thriving fishing industry. What else could a gruff old New Englander want? Nothing, as far as most townies were concerned.

"Shall I have someone show you to your room?" Gretta asked, getting Rose's check-in back on track.

"Yes. Where did that nice young man go?"

Gretta raised an eyebrow. "Who exactly?"

"The porter who brought in my bags."

"I'm sorry, ma'am—"

"Miss, thank you very much."

"What? Did you lose this one, too?" Frankie asked.

"Not that it's any of your business, but Signore Trevisani and I have parted ways."

Gretta didn't give them time to start going at each other again. "As I was saying, we don't employ a person in that role."

Rose looked perplexed, which was nearly a constant state of being for her. "Then who brought in my bags?"

"I believe you're referring to Mr. Bernardi."

"Penny's boy," Frankie explained. "He's the best man."

"How kind of him to help."

"As if he had a choice," Frankie said under her breath.

"Um," Rose said, attempting to look demure. "I still require someone to show me to my room."

Gretta dinged a small counterbell, and a scruffy man with a thick beard came out of the back office. "Chuck, please show this nice lady to her room."

Frankie chuffed. "Nice? Ha!"

"With all of that?" the man asked, pointing at Rose—not her luggage.

Gretta shot him a glance, and he slid through a hinged section of the counter without another word.

"Come on," he grumbled, grabbing a few bags and heading into the castle.

Rose shuffled after him. "I do love a man with strong arms."

"Do you now?" he asked, but didn't turn around.

"I wouldn't expect to see him for a while," Frankie said, pulling out rows of work, all the way back to the knit-two-purl-one she'd accidentally done when her sister first arrived.

Gretta picked up the brochure Rose hadn't taken with her and tossed it in the trash.

"I'm back," Val announced, appearing in the doorway and lifting her dress to show her undamaged hose.

"You missed all the action again, dear sister," Frankie said, not looking up.

"Fiddlesticks. Ooh, look who showed up."

3. No Croquembouche

"Watch yourself, Bianca," Tommy said, leading her up the uneven stone steps to the cloister—not that he could have caught her if she fell, being tipsy himself. The good thing was, he had lots of experience dealing with that sort of thing, working at the Top of the Harbor Hotel and Restaurant, so they managed to get to the landing without breaking their necks.

The steps weren't particularly weathered or worn. How could they be? They were located inside a building that had been completed in 1929. Like everything else in the castle, the steps had been intentionally built to appear like a pre-16th-century ruin. And considering the original owner's well-known penchant for hosting raucous dinner parties, it was a miracle people weren't regularly carted out the front door on stretchers.

These days, everyone who visited the castle gravitated to the cloister because it was so strange. The roof was made of glass, and the cobblestone walkway surrounding the central pool was decorated with facades of actual medieval buildings from throughout Europe. In other words, stepping into the cloister was like stepping back in time.

Behind Bianca, the matron of honor, Maisey Edmonds, clambered up the steps with a drink in one hand and her hiked-up dress in the other. "Whoever came up with bridesmaids' dresses should be shot. How am I supposed to get up these steps? I can't move my legs."

"Uh, that would be dudes," Tommy said, nodding his head approvingly. "Every guy knows bridesmaids' dresses never fit right. We're all hoping for a happy little accident. Know what I mean?"

Bianca slapped him on the arm. "Pervert!" But when he turned away, she snuck a glance to see if she'd inadvertently given him a show, not that the ticket would have cost much. She'd always been petite in every way, which was an asset on the sports field in high school but not great for getting noticed at the Windlass Bar and Grill. The only thing on her that was big was her waist-long dark-brown hair, styled into a single plait with beautiful flowers braided into it.

All in all, she liked the dress. It was a pretty color—a bright teal that complemented her hazel eyes—and it was convertible, so she'd be able to wear it again.

Satisfied that everything was where it was supposed to be, Bianca checked to see if Maisey had made it into the cloister yet.

Maisey's dress was teal and strapless, like hers, but the matron of honor hadn't opted for the convertible version. Hers was sleek from top to bottom, matching her slender body, and featured an elegant slit down the leg. This was because Maisey didn't need to wear dresses more than once, a perk of being married to Geoff Edmonds. There were tradeoffs, too, of course, but Maisey never complained, having grown up hand to mouth. That's how things were for a fisherman's daughter when your dad didn't own the boat. She didn't make a big deal about her newfound fortune, but it was evident that she was happy to have left poverty in the past.

Now she lived in a house far too big for two people. It even had a lawn tended by a team of landscapers who arrived every Friday morning to keep it looking its best for weekend parties. That was the life, as far as Bianca was concerned. Then again, Maisey would have plenty of work to keep her busy once the kids came along.

Geoff had made no secret of his desire for a large family. One of seven siblings, he was bound and determined to continue the tradition, just not yet. He wanted to wait until they were settled. Maisey often complained that she didn't know what that meant, considering how much more settled they were than her family had ever been, but the discussion was closed for now.

Maybe, Bianca thought, *if Geoff saw her in this gown, with her silky blonde hair done up with a crown of flowers, he'd be more amenable to getting started, but he was off on one of his business trips again.*

"Made it," Maisey said, spilling her drink. "A pool! I'd forgotten about that." She also temporarily forgot that her gown didn't permit running and almost fell headlong into the water. Luckily, a large stone box broke her fall. It was a sarcophagus for a small child. "Ew! That's creepy! The sculpture on top doesn't have a face."

"What does that mean?" Bianca asked, helping Maisey get back on her feet.

"No idea."

"And check out that gargoyle over there. I don't remember that. Has it always been here?"

"Must have been," Tommy said. "This place hasn't changed since the '30s." Tommy wasn't much taller than Bianca, but despite his slight build, he was very strong, having hauled many a fish out of Popplestone Harbor.

The three of them stood there, studying the grotesque gargoyle head spewing a never-ending stream of water into the pool. Its singular redeeming quality was that the sound of the fountain helped drown out Toni and Marco's arguing in the Wallpaper Room on the second floor.

With as much care as they could manage, having already raided the outside bar, the inside bar, and various minibars placed here and there, the girls kicked off their shoes and dipped their feet into the pool.

"This place is way stranger than I remember. Like a grown-up funhouse," Bianca said, tilting back so far that the wall behind her looked upside down. "It was fourth grade when we came here, right?"

Tommy sat down next to her, pulled off his socks, and rolled cuffs into his pant legs. "Something like that. It would make a wicked awesome haunted house!"

"You're so weird," Bianca said, kicking the water.

"Hey, watch it! You'll ruin my drink."

Maisey pointed at the ceiling. "It rains in here, right?"

"Yeah. It's like a greenhouse," Bianca said, studying the pipes above their heads. "There's a switch somewhere. I think that's how they water the plants."

Tommy made to get up and turn it on. "We've got to try that!"

"Don't you dare!" Maisey said, stopping him in his tracks.

Sitting back up, Bianca asked, "Who built this room, anyway? They must have been crazy."

"Or drunk," Tommy said, moving to investigate. "The storefronts were imported, right?"

"Watch out!" Bianca yelled. "You're going to fall in."

He'd taken a step back to get a better look and had inadvertently landed on the edge of the pool.

"Thanks," he said, winking at her. Then, he changed direction to explore the various businesses.

"I don't know why, but this pool makes me think about the time when the school shut down the men's swim team. Do you remember that?" Bianca asked.

Tommy chuckled. "Yeah, we were standing around naked because somebody swiped our clothes when we were in the showers. You should have seen the look on Ms. Baneck's face when we came out of the locker room in our birthday suits. I thought she was going to pop a blood vessel."

"It's a good thing she didn't see me standing behind you," Maisey said. "I was completely naked, too!"

The three of them nearly fell over laughing.

Doing his best to catch his breath, Tommy said, "I remember a group of guys standing in a circle to hide you."

"I don't think that's why they were so close to me," Maisey said, almost slipping into the pool as she rocked back and forth.

Tommy raised his glass. "You know what? We were pretty cool."

"Here, here!" Maisey agreed.

"The coolest," Bianca said, tipping her drink toward him. "To Popplestone High. After we left, it was never the same."

"To the swim team!" Tommy added, smacking his lips. "Amaretto makes me hungry. I wonder if there are any sausages in here?" He opened the door to a Bavarian shop and peeked in. "Nope, no sausages. What kind of restaurant is this anyway? Maybe I'll have better luck at the French pâtis-serie."

The girls continued chatting as Tommy searched for food in the faux storefronts.

"What was that kid's name?" Bianca asked, wracking her brain.

Maisey hadn't followed her friend's train of thought. "Who do you mean?"

"The guy who stole the clothing and hung it on the trees outside."

"They never found mine."

Bianca wrinkled her nose. "Ew! That's nasty. Did he keep it?"

"No idea. His name was…um…Marty. Marty Drinkwater."

"Yeah, that's the one. Whatever happened to him?"

Not paying attention to their conversation, Tommy said, "Nope, no *croquembouche*," closing another door. "It's a mu-seum in there with figureheads sticking out of the walls. This place is wild."

"I haven't the foggiest," Maisey said, ignoring Tommy. "He transferred."

Bianca got a wistful look in her eyes. "I thought he was kind of cute. And a good kisser."

"What?"

"You take what you can get when you can get it. Know what I mean? Even if it's in the baseball dugout after the game."

"I thought he used too much tongue," Maisey said under her breath, and they laughed again.

"Ah, Mediterranean!" Tommy exclaimed, making a beeline to the Italian ristorante in the hopes of placing an order for *spaghetti alla puttanesca*.

Out of nowhere, Bianca got serious. "I wish I had gotten out of here like Rose did."

Maisey was taken aback. "Are you kidding? You were the star of the field hockey team. You had a scholarship and were in the paper and everything."

"Nothin'," Tommy mumbled, closing the door.

"Whoop-de-doo," Bianca said. "I made the front page of the Popplestone Daily Times. I even remember the headline: *Local Athlete Scores Big!*"

"Hey, that's pretty special," Maisey said, looking slightly hurt.

"I guess, but where did it get me? Here I am, back on the island with no job, no guy, and no prospects. I might as well be in high school again."

"You could marry your cousin like Toni is doing," Tommy suggested, rejoining the conversation.

Bianca kicked the water again. "You're terrible!"

"In all seriousness, they aren't actually cousins, right?" Tommy asked, wandering over to the pool. "I mean, I know they aren't, but are they?"

"Of course not! They're cousins-in-law," Maisey said.

"No, no, no," Bianca corrected. "They're demi-sisters or semi-bros or something like that."

Maisey ran her finger around the top of her glass, making it sing. "Whatever it is, Tommy isn't wrong. It's a bit strange marrying your cousin."

Tommy put his hand over his heart and said, "I'd NEVER marry *my* cousin!"

"I would," Bianca said, immediately slapping her hand over her mouth.

"I'm telling him that!" Tommy yelled, pointing at her.

Bianca leapt to her feet and chased him around the room. "You better not!"

When she caught him, he turned the tables on her, threatening to throw her into the water.

"Oh, man. I just remembered how Marco and Toni used to sneak off during the football games," Maisey said, using her toe to trace the mosaic on the bottom of the pool.

Tommy loosened his grip on Bianca. "I remember that! Nothing says love like canoodling your cousin under the stands!"

Bianca took the opportunity to pull away, but not before stepping on his toe. "You're disgusting!"

"Ow! I won't deny it, but both of you are laughing!"

"I have an idea," Maisey said, getting to her feet.

Bianca threw out her hands as if to ward off danger. "Watch out, everyone. Maisey's got an idea!"

"Let's put the swim team back together. How about a dip?"

Bianca coughed as if she was choking on something. "Girl, are you crazy? What if we get caught? There are a hundred people out there waiting for the wedding to start."

But she was too late. Maisey had already stepped out of her dress and unclasped her strapless bra.

"I'm in," Tommy said, taking off his jacket. At that moment, a loud thump came from the second floor, and he looked up. "Sounds like they've worked things out. Maybe some pre-wedding makeup sex."

"Stop it!" Bianca scolded. "You know Toni made the pledge. It's her wedding day, and she hasn't even taken off the ring yet."

The thumping grew louder.

"She may be breaking her vow right this minute," Tommy said, pretending to search the floor. "Has anyone seen a ring lying around?"

Maisey rolled up her bra and stuck it into her bag. Then she slipped back into her dress. "I think we should check on them."

Tommy froze. "Are you nuts? You want to go up there and knock on the door? They might be—"

"—in trouble," Bianca finished for him. "That doesn't sound good."

"You go right ahead. I'm going to check if they have any food in this castle. Besides, that kind of thing is the best man's job. Where's Eddo anyway?"

Bianca pointed toward the great hall. "He went for a smoke."

Maisey climbed the stairs to the second floor. "I'm not waiting on him. I'll do it."

She stopped cold in her tracks when someone screamed so loudly the roof rattled. The three of them looked at each other and then charged upstairs to the room where their friends had been sequestered.

The mothers had chosen the Wallpaper Room because the two egresses were carefully hidden behind floral wallpaper. It was the perfect prank to play on drunk party-goers. They'd awake to find themselves in a room with no doors. Many a morning after had been met with yells for help emanating from the second-floor windows of the Bavarian sausage shop. But right now, the noises coming from that room sounded far more sinister.

Bang! Bang! Bang! Bang! Bang!

"Open up!" Maisey yelled, wailing on the door.

A final blood-curdling scream made their teeth chatter, and then silence.

"Oh, my God! They've killed each other!" Bianca said, bawling.

Maisey cursed as she paced back and forth. "Tommy, go find Marco's mom. Tommy! Are you listening? GO…GET… MARCO'S…MOM!"

A terrified Tommaso Amadeo Gentile stood motionless, his Italian margarita shaking in his hand.

"Now!" Maisey yelled.

He dropped the glass on the floor and tore down the steps.

"What do we do?" Bianca repeated over and over again.

"We get inside and see what's going on. That's what."

"But Maisey, what if they're dead? Like, really dead? Crumpled on the floor and dead!"

Maisey didn't want to think about that. She'd known Toni since preschool, and her best friend's life had been hard enough without this.

"Please, God. Don't let their bodies be cold and rigid," Bianca prayed.

Amplified by the narrow staircase, Frankie's gruff voice boomed down the hallway. "What's going on here?"

Behind her, Eddo and Tommy (who was still barefoot) followed at a safe distance.

"Toni and Marco were yelling and banging, and then they stopped," Bianca babbled.

Frankie pushed past the young women and banged on the door. "Marco? Toni?"

"What's wrong?" Val asked, huffing and puffing as she caught up to her sister.

Still sobbing, Bianca said, "Toni and Marco are…"

"They're what?"

"I'm trying to find out," Frankie snapped, pulling out an iron key Gretta gave her.

Everyone who rented the castle was provided with a key to the Wallpaper Room, just in case someone got locked in, intentionally or not.

Frankie slipped the key into the door lock and paused before giving it a turn. Then, she flung the door open and gasped. "For the love of God!"

Val fainted.

4. Brotherly Love

Across the castle grounds, people asked after the groom's father. No one knew why he was needed so urgently in the castle's great hall, but they fervently passed the message along, nevertheless.

"Have you seen Jimi?"

"No, he might be over at the wishing well."

"Isn't it romantic that Marco and Toni made their wish at the well just like Jimi and Frankie?"

"I guess, if you're into that kind of thing."

"I heard the wedding party was supposed to gather by the scenic overlook for photographs."

"That's after the wedding."

"Oh."

"Usually, it's the son, not the father, who goes missing right before the ceremony."

"Do you want another drink? It looks like this is going to take a while to get started."

"I wonder if the groom got cold feet."

"If I know Jimi—*and I know Jimi*—he'll talk some sense into that boy of his."

Unbeknownst to the gossiping attendees on the Magnolia Castle's sprawling lawn, Popplestone's indefatigable harbormaster was standing on the rocks, quietly contemplating the sea stretching out before him. He wasn't a tall man, standing only five feet six or so, but he had a powerfully stoic personality that kept people in line, especially during emergencies. It was one of the qualities that made him good at his job. Another was his inability to be swayed by cock-and-bull stories, which he heard a lot of from drunken pleasure seekers who didn't respect how dangerous boating and the ocean could be. When it came down to it, this was *his* harbor. He'd been master of its waterways for eleven years come August, and he couldn't imagine doing anything else.

This was why he'd walked down to the water's edge to get away from all the crazy happening back at the castle for a few blessed minutes. Once the ceremony was over, there'd be no escape from it—literally, because they'd be staying over to play a game about being locked in a dungeon or some fool thing—so he needed to soak up as much peacefulness as he could while he had the chance.

"Father," he said, not turning around.

"I hate it when you call me that," Father Abraham said, stepping alongside his brother like a shadow, covered from head to toe in black.

Both Amato brothers had red hair (though Abraham's was several shades darker), but that was where their similarities ended. Whereas Jimi was short and without affect, Abraham was tall and wore his heart on his sleeve. The most striking difference, however, was how they approached life. Jimi was a head-down, no-nonsense kind of person, while Abraham loved the pomp and circumstance that came with his station as a priest at Popplestone's Catholic Church.

"Quite the view," Abraham said, trying to start a conversation.

"No doubt."

"It looks like a storm's coming."

"Yup."

"Here, a server handed me this," Abraham said, offering his brother a drink. "Not my style. Do you want it?"

Jimi glanced down and held out his own glass. "Already have one."

Jimi was a man of few words, but Abraham was used to that. He'd been listening to his older brother's lack of sound his entire life and had long since learned to live with it.

"Caught a few stripers in that cove, didn't we?" the priest said more as a statement than a question, but surprisingly, he got an answer.

"Yup."

The cove off the castle's grounds contained one of the area's most notorious rock outcroppings (and one of the harbor's most popular fishing grounds). The vast majority of people knew Jonah's Reef from movies and poetry, but Jimi didn't concern himself with things like that. He focused on the people who'd lost their lives off the western shore and the families they'd left behind. Of course, the Coasties bunked in the Inner Harbor these days, but he still considered watching out for people the most important part of his job.

The brothers stood in silence for a while, listening to the water slap the guano-covered rocks.

Cormorants were Jimi's least favorite bird after the sky rats that mewed and cackled overhead. Then again, gulls were basically winged trash collectors eating anything that didn't kill them, which was a good thing. Otherwise, the place wouldn't just be covered with poop; there'd be a whole lot more rotting sea life, too.

Jimi knew the tourists and summer boarders didn't care much about the marine ecosystem, but he did. Funny how something could be irritating *and* remind you of how much you loved a place at the same time, not unlike going to a wedding.

Knowing full well that the conversation wouldn't continue without his help, Abraham said, "The lighthouse was prettier before they installed that radio tower. Now you can't take a picture of it from the breakwater without it getting in the way. Even from here, it blocks the view."

"Helps save lives," Jimi stated matter-of-factly.

"Of course, you're right. I'm sentimental. Speaking of which, I bet you're proud of your boy."

"Sure am."

"He knows how to pick 'em. Toni's a sweetheart."

"No doubt. She's smart not to marry a man of the sea."

"What do you mean?" Abraham asked.

"No one who works on the ocean is ever truly at home unless they're on a boat. I suppose Frankie knew that when we got married, but we never discussed it. Toni doesn't have anything to worry about, though. Marco's not about to step into his old man's shoes."

"I see."

"In a way," Jimi continued, "I've always thought Marco was more like you than me in that respect, but I don't see him following in either of our footsteps."

This caught Abraham off guard, but before he had a chance to respond, Gretta appeared.

"Excuse me, Father," she said, climbing down the rocky path. "Have you seen...oh...Mr. Amato. Just the man I'm looking for. You're needed inside."

"For what?"

"I wouldn't know. I was, however, asked to tell you that it's urgent."

"I'll be right in."

"If you'd come with me, that would be ideal," Gretta said, motioning toward the castle.

A long line of wedding attendees had gathered along the lawn's perimeter. A few had even taken the path to the Seaside Viewing Area, as the sign proudly stated, and were using the tower viewer to watch the three of them standing on the rocks.

Jimi was unmoved by her insistence that he leave the water's edge. "I'll be right in."

"I'll let them know," Gretta said, heading back.

Abraham looked extremely uncomfortable. "Sounds important. Shouldn't you find out what's wrong?"

"Is that a little Fatherly advice?" Jimi asked his very tall little brother.

"No. It's just that I've done a few of these before, and I'm familiar with how tense people get. I usually find it better to head things off at the pass than to let them fester."

"I see."

They stood in silence for a while longer as more people gathered to see what was happening.

Once again, Abraham spoke first. "How does it not get to you?"

"Them?" Jimi asked, nodding his head toward the eager onlookers.

"Yes."

"Well, Abe, I live my life in a fishbowl. I can't take a piss at the Windlass without someone yelling at me for pulling their mooring or breakin' a cleat after I towed 'em in. So you'll forgive me—which is your job, by the way—for not jumping every time someone lights a fire. The water's a dangerous enough place without overreacting every time there's a minor emergency."

"I can understand that," Abraham said, obviously feeling uncomfortable with everyone staring at two of them. "My job's no easier, you know."

"No, it isn't, but you don't have to see people when they're confessing. I have to look folks in the eye when I sit next to them at the bar."

"I have an idea. Why don't I go in and see what's going on? You can wait here until I get back."

"Nope. I do my own work," Jimi said, but he didn't leave. "Besides, do you want to be the one to get in the way when Frankie, Val, or both are on the warpath?"

Abraham grimaced. He knew precisely how fiery the Bellagamba sisters could be, having been affianced to Val before taking the cloth.

"JAMES AMATO!" Frankie's voice bellowed out of the castle. "GET IN HERE!"

"That's my cue," Jimi said, handing his drink to Abraham.

He hated cocktails, but they were part of his wife's plan for the day. *No beer,* she'd said. *I've selected an almond-themed catering service. It'll be lovely.*

"If you enjoy froufrou girlie drinks with no kick and everything being sweet, I guess," Jimi mumbled aloud.

"What's that?" Abraham asked. He hadn't wanted one of the light-weight drinks; now he had two.

"Nothing. Say a prayer for me."

Abraham placed the glasses on a waiting table and said, "That, I can do."

As Jimi walked across the lawn between the Bellagamba side and the Bellagamba-Amato side, many eyes followed his progress toward the castle, and many tongues wagged.

For two and a half hours, the guests had waited under the blazing summer sun, and people's nerves were wearing thin. Arguments had broken out about the usual things: football, politics, who cheated on whom with whom when their partner was at the Windlass arguing about football and politics. People were tired. They were hungry. And, most importantly, they were drunk. It was the perfect recipe for disaster.

Then, someone said what everyone was thinking, and things got out of hand.

"This is all Marco's fault!" someone yelled.

"No way. Not Marco."

"If anyone's to blame, it has to be Toni."

"Why would you say that? Toni's a sweetheart."

"She's the one who broke it off with him last year before they got back together."

"Yeah, but don't you remember? Marco dated that Vivisani girl? Toni never dated anyone else."

"Are you sure about that? It's only a ring after all, not a chastity belt."

"How dare you!"

Such is the way when one lives in a small community. Every sordid detail is common knowledge, especially where relationships were concerned. Soon, the gossip escalated into insults, and a brawl ensued.

The professional wrestling world would have been proud. Aunties in floral maxi dresses whacked people with their parasols, drinks were thrown in people's faces, and fistfuls of food from the reception tables were lobbed at unsuspecting distant relatives.

Everything came to a head when the cake table tumbled over, and the bride and groom figurines landed on the ground with a resonant splat.

• • • • •

"Exactly how did you lose your children on their wedding day?" Jimi asked, showing more emotion than he'd displayed in years.

"They were talking about calling off the wedding, so we locked them in the Wallpaper Room to work things out," Frankie explained.

"You did what?" he asked, running his hand through his ginger hair.

Red hair wasn't terribly common for people with their heritage, but it wasn't unheard of either. Deep down, Jimi hoped his grandkids would have it, too…and it could happen because Toni and Marco both had red hair. That made it a better-than-even chance, despite being a recessive trait.

"You were in on this, too, Val?" he asked.

The middle Bellagamba sister didn't answer. She was too busy collapsing in a corner.

Jimi returned to questioning his wife. "And you opened the door, which was locked with no other way out, and they weren't in there?"

Frankie pointed at Eddo.

"Turns out there *is* another way out. There's a secret hatch in the floor that leads to a set of stairs," Eddo said, lifting a corner of the well-worn rug.

"Anyone go down it yet?" Jimi asked.

"Yeah, I did," Tommy said. "It leads to the first floor. There are exits into the great hall, the dining room, and outside. They could be anywhere."

"Great. Just great," Jimi mumbled, pushing his way past everyone to inspect the secret hatch himself. "I suppose we should find them. I'm open to suggestions on where to look."

Tommy coughed. "There are a lot of rooms in this place!"

"Not helpful," Frankie said, and Tommy shut his mouth.

Bong! Magnolia Castle's bell tower chimed.

Jimi let the trap door fall back into place. "Now what?"

It chimed two more times, and the string quartet began to play.

"Out of my way!" Frankie yelled. "No one is starting this wedding without me."

"How exactly are we planning to have a wedding without a bride and groom?" Jimi asked no one in particular.

Eddo shrugged and sauntered down the stairs ahead of him.

5. Trapped In A Dungeon

"What in the world is going on out here?" Jimi exclaimed, stepping out of the castle.

Startled by the ringing of the bell, the brawling guests had stopped mid-bludgeon, frozen like a Baroque painting of the descent into hell. The only person still moving under the tent was Gretta, feverishly trying to put things right.

Much to Jimi's surprise, Frankie appeared entirely unfazed. Her son was getting married today, and that was all that mattered. Fixing her thinning hair, she continued with the proceedings as if nothing was out of the ordinary.

"It's a disaster," Jimi said, trying to get her attention.

"No, no, no," she said, ignoring his assessment of the situation. "You have to stay here, remember? You're going to walk Toni down the aisle."

"What aisle?"

Frankie shot him a withering glance.

"I'm just saying, watch your step. You wouldn't want to trip on someone lying face down in the dirt."

"Tommy!" she demanded, thrusting out her elbow. "Show me to my seat."

A pale-faced Tommy stepped over the remnants of the wedding cake, making sure not to squash the figurines lying on the ground, and took Frankie's arm.

As they promenaded through the mayhem, the groom's mother greeted people, paying no attention to the torn dresses, black eyes, or overturned chairs. "Nice to see you. Thank you for coming. Oh, isn't what's left of your corsage lovely?"

"She's a trooper," Jimi remarked proudly as he watched his wife strut through the shocked wedding guests.

As the wedding party marched by, Gretta tried to get everyone back into their seats.

Still reeling from the effects of passing out, Eddo basically had to carry Val to her overturned seat. Once she was situated, he assumed his position to Father Abraham's left.

"You have the ring, correct?" the priest asked out of the side of his mouth.

Eddo patted his pockets, raised a finger as if to say *wait a minute*, and jogged to his car to retrieve it.

"Forgot the ring?" Jimi asked as he passed.

The best man shrugged and kept going.

With a celebratory flourish, the castle's rear doors opened, and the music changed.

Maisey and Bianca emerged, wobbling a little as they descended a staircase that led to the lawn and giggling the entire way. Unlike the cloister's steps, these were shallower and wider to prevent any mishaps. Even so, Bianca managed to trip, but no one noticed or seemed to care. Finally, Toni appeared in the doorway, carrying a bouquet of sweet almond verbena flowers and glowing like every happy bride should on their wedding day.

She was a vision of beauty. Her red hair was tied with a lovely floral circlet around a neat bun. She wore a one-shoulder dress adorned with shimmering beads that extended down to her wrist on the left side. On the right, her arm and shoulder were completely bare, revealing her precious butterfly birthmark.

Jimi whistled. "You look stunning."

"Thank you, Uncle Jimi."

"I'm glad you're okay, but you do know your aunt is going to kill you after the service, right?" he said, taking her arm.

"Since I've already been dead once today, what's one more time going to matter?"

Jimi's face said, *That's not funny,* but she laughed and kissed him on the cheek.

Holding the crook of her arm out to him, she said, "Besides, she'll have to catch us first. We're heading out right after dinner."

"I forgot. You aren't staying for that escape room thingamajig. Good for you. I'd get as far away from this place as humanly possible."

"We're planning on it."

Toni beamed a great big smile as she walked toward the wedding arbor, which was festively adorned with flowers and ribbons. In the background, the string quartet struck up the bridal procession, and everyone who still could, stood.

Ahead of her, Marco slipped in from the side, followed by Eddo.

• • • • •

After the service, only a few people stayed for the reception. Why bother? Most of the food was on the ground, and no one needed more to drink after waiting so long for the ceremony to begin.

As the wedding party posed in various configurations in front of the scenic overlook—a series of stone archways opening to Popplestone Harbor—attendees didn't bother waving goodbye before climbing the uneven stairs toward the main, street-level parking lot. Most looked a little worse for wear, and many had damaged presents under their arms, having retrieved them from the overturned gift table. Toni and Marco couldn't keep a straight face for the photos because they found it so amusing.

"That's a wedding for the books," Tommy said, standing beside Eddo, who'd returned to his natural state of leaning against the bell tower.

The photographer was currently working on mother/daughter pictures, so the men had the chance to sneak off for a few minutes.

"It ain't over yet," Eddo said, pulling out his half-finished cigarette and relighting it. "They have to sign the papers. So, I'll need that stuff I gave you to hold for me."

"Yeah, right. I'll get it." Dashing off, Tommy headed to his car to retrieve the pen and inkwell that Eddo had asked him to keep earlier in the day.

When he returned, it didn't look like Eddo had moved a muscle. He was still leaning against the portico like James Dean.

"Here," Tommy said, handing an old box in the shape of a treasure chest to the best man.

"Thanks."

Frankie clapped her hands. "All right. Let's head over to the drawbridge."

Tommy frowned, dropping the cigarette he'd just lit to the ground and grinding it into the macadam with the toe of his wingtips. "Once more into the fray."

"I'll be right there. I need to give this to Father Abraham," Eddo said, trotting off.

Now that six thousand nine hundred and forty-seven pictures of the proceedings had been safely stored on duplicate SD cards, the wedding party prepared to take more photos.

"This is ridiculous," Jimi mumbled, helping Val along the path to the castle's main entrance.

"Zip it," Frankie said, passing him with the photographer in tow. "This way. You have your camera, right? I want a picture of everyone crossing the drawbridge and then another as they step through the doors into the castle. And don't forget to take one of the entire wedding party on the grand steps inside."

The photographer grunted and waved to her assistant, who looked like a pack mule weighed down with bags of lenses and assorted camera equipment. In each hand, he carried a tripod with a battery-powered LED light on top.

As they waited their turn, everyone mingled among the flowers and manicured topiary. One particularly naughty sculpture drew many laughs from the younger members of the group, but Frankie wouldn't let them take a picture with it for the wedding book. The bell tower, which had been rung to begin the service, stood silently off to the side, dwarfed by the monolithic stone edifice that was Magnolia Castle. Adding to the effect, the building was surrounded by a shallow moat lined with a wide array of blue flowers representing water, and several large rhododendrons guarded the bridge.

One by one, Frankie directed everyone to pose for two pictures: one serious photo and one in which they made faces or pretended to recoil in fear of a troll emerging from under the bridge. Afterward, Gretta asked them to place their phones, smartwatches, and other personal electronic devices into a lockbox and invited them into the castle. To no one's surprise, it didn't go as planned.

Toni nearly fell into the flower-moat when Marco moved the wrong way. Bianca hiked her dress so high that Frankie had to adjust it before she'd let the picture be taken. And Rose had to be frisked because one of her breasts had a strange rectangular shape to it. After removing a phone hidden in her bra, one in her garter, and a smartwatch without a strap tucked into an unmentionable place, she was finally allowed to proceed.

When it looked like no one was left, Gretta asked Frankie if they were finished.

"I think so. I hope we didn't miss anyone."

Gretta moved to close the castle's magnificent carved doors when a person wearing colorful scrubs came running down the steps from the car park.

"Wait for me!" the nurse yelled, speeding toward them. When she reached the bridge, she tripped and spilled her oversized bag on the ground.

Frankie helped gather her things. "I'm glad you made it. Toni will be thrilled."

"Almost didn't, apparently."

Reading the cover of one of the books that fell out of her friend's bag, Frankie said, "*Ms. Prissy Langenshire's Guide to Figuring Out If You've Been Murdered.* Really?"

"You haven't lived if you haven't read it. Besides, for all we know, one of us could have been murdered and we just don't know it yet!"

They laughed.

"You know we'll be busy with the escape room tonight, right?" Frankie asked. "I doubt you'll have much time for reading."

"It doesn't matter. I don't go anywhere without Ms. L!"

"You and those books."

"Murder, mystery, intrigue? What's not to like?"

Frankie handed her friend the novel, and they headed in.

• • • • •

The doors closed with a bang that echoed through the stone corridors.

"That sounded rather final," Bianca said, stepping closer to Tommy.

That was fine with him. He very much hoped to find a secluded corner to spend some quality time with her later in the evening.

Frankie did her best to corral everyone onto the staircase that led to the great hall. After much jostling and several bright flashes from the photographer's camera, they were finally released from their duties.

Jimi sighed. "I'm glad that's over."

"You wish," Rose said, looking for the bar. "We're going to be stuck in here all night, remember?"

"I haven't forgotten."

"Auntie Christine!" Toni said, throwing her arms around the late arrival.

They weren't related, but Toni had referred to the nurse that way since childhood. In actual fact, Christine lived next door and was more family than most of the people who'd attended the ceremony.

"I'm sorry I missed it. I got held over on my shift at the hospital."

"How many people did you save today?" Toni asked, leading Christine to the dinner table.

"Being a nurse isn't that glamorous. You'd probably lose your lunch if I told you the things I did today."

"Don't worry. I haven't eaten," Toni said, laughing and moving off to chat with someone else.

Chuck, the gruff man who'd—among other things—helped Rose to her room, banged a small gong.

The youngest Bellagamba sister winked at him, but Chuck pretended not to notice. He was too busy fixing his shirt, which he realized was buttoned incorrectly.

"If I could have your attention, please," Gretta said, addressing the wedding party. "Welcome to *Trapped in a Dungeon*, Magnolia Castle's premiere escape room adventure."

Everyone except Rose clapped. The enjoyable effects of being frisked had worn off, and she was sore about being required to give up her electronic devices.

"From this moment on," Gretta continued, "you will be challenged to find a way out. You have until dawn."

"And when exactly is that?" Rose asked.

"5:09 a.m.," Jimi answered without missing a beat.

"Figures you'd know."

Gretta did her best to smile. "Should you need assistance for any reason, Father Abraham has access to a panic button that communicates with the outside and unlocks the exits. But don't expect him to end the game without good reason. Once he raises the alarm, the experience is over, and everyone will be escorted from the premises. Understood? Good."

"She's a bit stiff, isn't she?" Bianca asked Tommy under her breath.

"Yeah. Cold as ice. Not warm and cuddly like you."

Bianca elbowed him in the side.

"Ow!"

"I wonder if she's really like that or if it's an act," she asked.

"Don't know, but I like it. It kind of adds to the whole experience."

"Definitely."

Gretta continued her explanation. "The bride and groom will stay for dinner. After which time, there will be a signing ceremony, and they'll leave. At that point, the doors will be locked, and the game will commence. Are you ready? Excellent. Let's begin. Will the bride and groom please sit at either end of the table as is customary in King Radimir's court? Next are their parents: Ms. Bellagamba here, beside the bride, and Mr. and Mrs. Amato at the other end. Mrs. Amato on Marco's right. Yes. That's correct. And Mr. Amato, on his left, followed by the best man, groomsman, and Father Abraham. On the bride's side: the matron of honor, bridesmaid, Miss Trevisani, and honored guest."

"Her name is Christine," Toni whispered.

"Ms. Christine, then. Your accommodations have been prepared. If you'll please see me after dinner, I will give you your key. Now, is everyone situated?"

Tommy reached for a roll, but Bianca kicked his leg under the table. "What? I'm hungry?"

"Good things come to those who wait," she whispered.

Tommy looked perplexed and then smiled.

A peal of thunder rumbled through the castle, and everyone looked toward the sky.

"Is that part of the experience, too?" Rose asked.

Gretta rolled her eyes as she removed a scroll from a display case. It was decorated with gold leaf and had red tassels on its ends.

She read, "You and your party have been summoned here by the king to make the castle safe for his arrival. It has come to his attention that the evil Count Mountebane has hatched a plot to assassinate him by placing a trap somewhere on the premises. Your job is to find and disarm this insidious device before he arrives tomorrow. Once you are done eating, you'll find your first clue hidden under the serving plate. But take care, or *you* will be the one to fall prey to Count Mountebane's dastardly plan."

Chuck rang the gong again, only this time, it sounded ominous. Suddenly, the weapons hanging on the walls, suits of armor, and the blazing fire in the oversized fireplace looked dangerous in the flickering light.

Gretta replaced the scroll and said, "Dinner is served."

6. The Clue

"I quite enjoyed that," Father Abraham announced, pushing back from the table, "but I must excuse myself."

"Don't you want to read the clue with us?" Toni asked.

She and Marco weren't staying for the evening's festivities, but she wanted to see what it was going to be like. Toni had always been one for games—especially the kind that involved strategizing with a group of players. One day, she hoped to head up a think tank or organize team-building activities at some mega business, but for now, she'd settle for the first clue of their escape room adventure.

"I'm afraid games aren't my forte, my child. Besides, I'll be right over there, preparing the documents to make your nuptials official."

"I thought it *was* official," she said, poking at the vegetables left on her plate. Toni was into games, yes. Asparagus? No.

"In the eyes of the Lord, you most certainly are; however, according to our illustrious legal system, we're not quite there yet. But don't worry. We'll remedy that with a few well-placed pen strokes."

Father Abraham stood, nodded his head to Toni and Marco, and pushed in his chair. He then retrieved a bag he'd stashed behind the pulpit at the far end of the hall.

Fashioned in the shape of an eagle with outstretched wings, this particular lectern was one of his favorites. He felt it was fitting for a medieval-style castle to have a pulpit, given the importance of religion to Europeans at the time. However, he was equally glad the castle's builders hadn't adopted other aspects of medieval life, such as a lack of indoor plumbing and the Black Death.

Stepping through an opening in the short wall surrounding the podium, he ran his fingers over the eagle's golden wings and paused. He enjoyed imagining the hall filled with an attentive congregation hanging on his every word.

In his mind, he delivered his favorite sermon: Exodus 20. He'd been revising that particular oration recently, and he almost had it where he wanted it. Unfortunately, he wouldn't get the chance to present it to his parishioners for a while, since that sermon was scheduled for the Third Sunday of Lent: *The Covenant of the Ten Commandments*.

"An oldie but goodie," he mumbled before turning around.

Interestingly, the lectern boasted another unique feature Abraham wished was common to all of the places where he preached: a hidden door that led to other areas of the castle. More than once, he'd used it to slip away from the near-constant chaos that accompanied weddings and other services. He even had a flask stashed in a dark corner of the tunnel, which he intended to retrieve at the next opportunity. But first, he needed to locate the license papers and prepare them for the signing ceremony.

After Abraham left the table, almost everyone else got up, too.

"Wait, we have to read the clue," Toni insisted, making a second attempt to start the game.

"How about we let our stomachs settle first," Jimi suggested, heading to the patio. "I need some fresh air before we're locked into this place for the night. Would you like to come with me, son?"

"Sure," Marco said, knowing it wasn't a request. He'd been expecting a talking to about the day's events ever since they'd finished taking pictures. Before leaving, he kissed Toni on the forehead and said, "Looks like I'm not the only one being summoned to a conference. Mom's on her way over."

Toni sighed. "Best get this over with."

Frankie took her son's bride by the hand and led her away. "Val, are you coming?"

"Maybe later," the middle Bellagamba sister answered, letting Frankie and her daughter move to a connecting room without her. Val remained at the table until everything except for the clue had been cleared away by Gretta and Chuck, reserving a tall glass of wine (the only beverage besides coffee that didn't contain amaretto) and a plate of almond cookies for herself.

"Hey, are we allowed to play it?" Tommy asked, sitting at the organ situated at the other end of the hall.

"Don't touch it. You'll get us in trouble," Bianca said, pulling the flowers out of her hair. They'd had a long day, and they were looking weary.

Tommy lifted his hands anyway, as if to slam them on the keys, and Gretta appeared out of nowhere.

"I'll thank you not to touch the organ," she said before launching into the remarks she'd prepared for the castle's tour guides. "We maintain this magnificent instrument for concerts and services, and one must be approved before being allowed to play it. You see, it represents the pinnacle of mid-century American organ construction. Not only is it the largest organ on the continent, but it also sports ranks of pipes constructed by a surprisingly comprehensive list of contemporary organ builders, making it utterly unique."

Bianca slapped Tommy. "I told you not to touch it."

He sheepishly slid off the bench, replacing the red velvet rope he'd moved out of the way. "Sorry."

Bianca pulled Tommy through a curtain as red as the rope into the short hallway connecting the lobby to the tower and the great room. Speaking quietly, she said, "I have a better game to play."

"What's that?" Tommy asked, leaning against a vending machine, still recuperating from the shock of Gretta's apparition-like manifestation.

"Wouldn't you like to know, but you'll have to find me first before I tell you."

"Like hide-and-seek?"

"Um, more along the lines of I hide, and you find the surprise waiting for you. When you do, you'll be very happy."

"That sounds like a fun game, but what about the escape room?"

"I promise this will be infinitely more entertaining," she said, disappearing through the velvet curtain.

Tommy heard her muffled voice from the other room. "Finders keepers, as they say."

Wringing his hands, he counted, "One, two, three…wait a minute. What number do I count to?"

When he got no answer, he peeked through the archway to see which direction Bianca went.

"What are you doing?" Maisey asked, noticing the disembodied head poking through the curtain.

"Playing a game with Bianca, I think."

"Hide-and-find, I bet."

"How did you know?"

"I've known Bianca for a long time. It's one of her favorite games; that and dare-and-dare. Better get going. She doesn't like to be kept waiting."

Tommy hesitated for a moment, imagining all of the possibilities of what Bianca had in store for him. Then, unable to bear the suspense anymore, he took off after her.

Maisey gazed at the rows of organ pipes towering above them, trying to catch a glimpse of the elaborate rose window in the wall, but she couldn't see it from this angle. "If only you were here, Geoff," she said, wishing he hadn't been called away on urgent business. Of course, business was *always* urgent, and lately, she'd begun to worry that he liked going on trips more than being at home. While he flew first class to

Paris or Frankfurt—even a place called Dubai somewhere in the Middle East—she was forced to wait patiently in Popplestone for his return.

Snapping out of her reverie, she said, "I'm going to freshen up. Ms. Bellagamba, would you like to accompany me to the powder room?"

"No, thank you, dear," Val answered. "I'm not quite finished yet."

Maisey didn't like walking around the castle alone, but nature was calling, so she headed to the restroom. As she walked by the suit of armor guarding the stairs to the castle's entrance, she tapped it on the nose plate and said, "No peeking."

When Father Abraham finally lifted his eyes from the pulpit, he saw Val slumped in a chair, snoring gently. "Not unlike Sunday morning," he said, chuckling.

"I know I haven't led a perfect life," he said, looking up at the rose window. The dense cloud cover prevented the stars and moon from illuminating it from the outside, making it look gray and lifeless. "But I've tried to atone for my sins. I've dedicated my life to you and the church. Is that enough? I guess, someday I'll find out, but until then, a sign that I'm on the right path would be nice."

But Abraham knew that prayer didn't work that way. After a few seconds with no response, he sighed, resigned to waiting until he stood before the pearly gates to hear Saint Peter's verdict.

He was so deep in thought that he didn't notice Eddo appear next to him, and he jumped. "Oh, it's you, my son. I see you're familiar with the hidden passageway, too."

"Before Dad put me to work on the boat, I used to play here on Saturdays when my mom worked in the front office. Sometimes, I'd pop out and scare people."

"Sounds fun," Abraham said doubtfully. "I see you've brought me something."

"Yeah, here." Eddo handed Father Abraham an ornate pen and inkwell. "Jimi gave this to me as the best man. He said it was important that Toni and Marco sign with this pen, but he didn't tell me why."

"It's an Amato tradition," Abraham explained. "Parents from both sides put ink in the well. Then, when the bride and groom use it to sign the license, it symbolizes the union of their families. Every Amato for generations has formalized their nuptials with this pen, except me. I forfeited any chance of that when I became a priest."

"Sorry," Eddo said.

"Don't be. Accepting this path was a calling and not one I took lightly. Believe you me, I had plenty of opportunities to go a different way. In the end, this was the correct path."

"Uh-huh," Eddo grunted, unconvinced the priest was telling the truth. "I've got to..." he pointed in the other direction.

"Of course. Thank you for bringing this to me. I'll make good use of it."

Eddo nodded before vaulting over the short stone wall surrounding the alcove where the pulpit resided.

"Oh, to be that nimble," Abraham said, pulling off the pen's ornate, golden cap.

When he dipped the nib into the well and pulled the lever to fill the pen with ink, it exploded all over his hands.

"Bugger. Good thing I hadn't taken out the license yet, or I'd be running to the parish to grab another one. I'd better wash up," he thought to himself.

Holding his hands out so he didn't get ink on anything, he pushed through the hinged door that closed off the alcove from the rest of the hall and found his way to the kitchen.

Since that space was usually off-limits to patrons, he hoped no one would discover his faux pas, and he could return to his duties before anyone noticed he was missing. Priests, after all, weren't supposed to be clumsy.

7. Brewing Storm

Frankie huffed, exasperated by the interruption. "No, Tommy, Bianca is not in here. You'd think she'd have grown out of playing games by now."

Toni giggled, covering her mouth with her hand.

"What are you laughing at?" Frankie asked, turning back to Val's daughter.

"Oh, nothing."

Frankie and her niece, now daughter-in-law, had retreated to a small room off the main stairs into the great hall. It was the most private place Frankie knew of beyond going to her room in the servants' wing, but she had no intention of putting that much distance between herself and the proceedings. This would provide enough privacy for what she needed to say.

The door had a polished brass plaque with the words *Bridal Room* written in a frilly script. The room itself housed a wide array of wedding paraphernalia used to show off past events and provide brides with options for their big day—or little day, as the case may be, because the castle also offered the popular *Le Petit Mariage* package for couples on a budget.

Toni, who was still wearing her wedding dress, blended seamlessly with her surroundings.

"I don't understand," Frankie said, keeping her voice low. "Why would you do that to your mother and me? It's not like you. You've always been the considerate one."

"You locked me in a room, Aunt Frankie. What did you expect me to do?"

"Because you were threatening to cancel the wedding! Do you have any idea how much this cost? Money doesn't grow on trees. The whole family chipped in, and then you come to us saying you want to call it off?"

"We didn't say that," Toni said, starting to get upset. "We just needed a break from all of this."

"All of what?"

"You, okay? You! Every minute it's: *Do this! Be here! Take this over there!* This was supposed to be OUR wedding day. You made it a production."

Stung by her niece's words, Frankie collapsed into a white lace-covered chair. "It *was* your day, but weddings take a lot of planning. I wanted to make it special. A day you'd remember for the rest of your lives."

"You certainly did that."

"No, you don't understand. Jimi and I had to deal with a lot when we got married. I didn't want that to happen to you. That's why I helped as much as I could."

"But that's just it, Aunt Frankie, you weren't helping. You stressed us out."

"Being married *is* being stressed. Besides, what was I supposed to think when you two started arguing?"

"Nothing."

"What?"

"Nothing. It's not your place to think about my relationship with Marco. It's ours and ours alone. And if we decide to take a break or whatever, that's fine because it's what we want."

Frankie straightened a lovely crocheted throw draped over the chair's arm. "I don't understand."

"I know."

"I was so worried."

"You don't need to worry about us. Marco loves me, and I love him. We're going to be together forever. Who knows, maybe our kids will get married right here, and you can make their lives miserable, too."

Frankie sputtered. "But I—"

"I'm kidding. Come here. Besides, it wouldn't be much of an escape-themed wedding if the bride and groom didn't escape the room they were locked in, would it?"

Frankie tried to smile, but her face twisted into a pained expression.

"The truth is, Marco and I appreciate how much you've done. It just got a little much there for a minute or two, but now things are better."

"Are you sure?"

"Absolutely. And we're married!" Toni said, displaying her ring.

"It's beautiful. And so are you. Do you mind if we sit here a minute?" Frankie asked, not ready to give up the nicest moment she'd had with her niece in ages. "No need to rush. Abe isn't going anywhere."

"That's the best thing you've suggested all day. Thank you, Aunt Frankie. I love you."

"Love you too, little butterfly."

· · · · ·

After scouring the castle for Bianca, Tommy found himself back where he began, standing in the hallway outside the tower entrance.

A sign had been hung on the handle at a jaunty angle, which he read. "*Off Exhibit. No Admittance.* Hmm. Then why are you unlocked?"

Tommy reached for the barred door, and it swung open. He hesitantly peeked in. "Hello?"

When no one appeared, he breathed a sigh of relief. He'd half expected Gretta to jump out and frighten the life out of him.

"Just a drafty old castle, I guess. Let's see if you hid in here, Bianca," he said, slipping into the darkness.

Unable to see, Tommy groped the wall for some indication of the space's shape. His hand landed on a switch, and he flipped it. "Ah ha!"

A thin line of lights stretched around the corner, following the circular stone staircase to the top of the tower.

"Up we go," he announced, but he only made it a few steps before coming face to face with a second barred gate set into the tower wall. It was the castle's dungeon!

"How cool is this?" he said, peering through the bars. "Dang. Not cool at all!"

Within the confines of the cell, a skeleton lay draped across a decaying bed.

"Yuck. That's disgusting. I hope it isn't real."

He almost went back but figured he might not get another chance to explore the tower, especially if Gretta caught him, so he continued up the stairs to the next level. It proved to be worthwhile.

Although Bianca wasn't there, he did find cases of jewel-encrusted daggers carefully preserved in glass cabinets, fans of swords adorning the walls, and two suits of armor waiting at the ready on either side of a velvet throne.

"Super cool," he said, lifting a sword and shield propped against the wall. With a lofty air, he sat on the throne and pretended to be King Radimir. "Off with his head!" he commanded, swinging the sword and accidentally hitting the pike staff held by one of the suits of armor.

He watched helplessly as it toppled onto the ground with a crash. Removing himself from the throne, he gingerly propped the sword and shield against the wall, placed the pike staff back in the suit of armor's hands, and tiptoed out of the room. In case someone—namely, Gretta—had heard, he headed to the third level, where he planned to wait until it was safe to sneak back to the great hall.

It turned out that the top floor was a simple chapel with religious tapestries on the walls, a prayer bench, and an altar.

"Sorry. Didn't mean to interrupt," he said, staring at a long pole topped with a crucifix. Making the sign of the cross, he bowed his head and backed out.

"Is anyone messing around up there?" Gretta called from below.

"Shoot. Busted," he whispered, but didn't respond.

"I'm glad no one disregarded my sign because if a person were to find themselves locked in there, it might be weeks before anyone discovered the body. It's totally soundproof. I mean, who would want to listen to people in the dungeon moaning from lack of food and water all night long?"

Tommy practically flew down the steps. "Wait, wait, I'm here, don't lock me in!"

When he reached the bottom, Gretta slammed the gate, barring his exit. From the outside, she stared at him with eyes so cold that Tommy shivered.

Pointing to a heavy metal door painted an ominous black, she asked, "Give me one good reason why I shouldn't shut this door and be done with you?"

"Listen. It's not what you think. There's this girl—"

"Hold it right there. It's exactly what I think. And I don't want to hear it. This is strike two. If I catch you messing around one more time, I'll go all medieval on you, and I've got access to the tools to do it. Just look around. Hmm. Maybe you can be our new skeleton."

Tommy went white.

"Capiche?"

"Yeah, got it," he said, vigorously nodding and pointing to the door. "Now, let me out."

"No more snooping. Go to the great hall. Read the clues. Play the game. That's what you're here for, not nookie in the dungeon with your girlfriend."

"She's not my girlfriend. We were just fooling around."

"Too much information. Go," Gretta said, pulling on the barred door and pointing to the curtain that led back to the great hall.

"No more snooping for me. Uh-uh. No way," he said, rushing by her. "Man, Bianca is going to be pissed when I don't find her."

Gretta slammed the door. Then she replaced the chain and padlock that had been removed earlier that day because a cat had found their way in. Chuck had retrieved the animal, but clearly had forgotten to lock up after himself.

Most of the time, they left the outer steel door open, allowing people to peer through the bars. Tonight, she shut it with a clank and locked it behind her. She'd have to speak with Chuck about being more careful, or the insurance folks would shut them down for good.

• • • • •

Marco and Jimi stood on the patio, gazing at the harbor.

A lifetime of experience told Marco that his father had something to say, but also that he wouldn't be the first to speak, so he broke the ice. "It's been looking like a storm's coming all day."

"Yup."

"Shouldn't you be out there?"

"What good is it to have an assistant harbormaster if they sit in the office all day. Max can handle it."

Marco looked at his father. "You don't believe that, do you?"

"Nope. That kid's as green as grass, but the Coasties will look after him."

As was often the case when talking to Jimi, they stood in silence for several minutes before Marco couldn't take it anymore and said something. "Do you remember that night we came home from fishing, and the water was flat as a mirror?"

"Yup."

"It reflected the sunset and was so smooth the boat slipped sideways when we made turns in the creek."

"Sure did."

"I wish we could go back to that. Things were much simpler back then."

Jimi turned to his son and put a hand on his shoulder. "That's because you were ten."

It wasn't a comforting thought.

Christine appeared behind them, stepping onto the patio. "Wow, such a moody night. I wonder if it's going to rain. Oh, sorry. I didn't realize you were still here. I'll head inside."

"Nonsense," Jimi said, surveying the harbor he'd sworn to protect. "What's the point of living in a place like this if you don't share it?"

Marco was surprised by his father's response. He'd never known the man to be prone to bouts of nostalgia.

"It *is* beautiful, isn't it?" Christine asked, stepping to the railing and peering down the coastline toward the fort. Its cannons had recently been restored, but she hadn't had a chance to see them yet. "Even on a night like this, it's hard to imagine the terrible things that have happened on those rocks," she said, pointing toward the water. "How many ships have been lost on Jonah's Reef?"

"Too many," Jimi answered.

The air grew heavy with the oncoming storm, and Jimi looked out at the sea. The only light came from Sandy Bar Lighthouse on the eastern shore. Round and round its light searched the sea for wayward ships, passing over the open ocean, the breakwater, the western shore, the harbor, up the eastern shore, and out to sea again.

"I'll leave you to it," Christine said, not wanting to overstay her welcome.

A distant rumble reached their ears, and a few heavy raindrops struck the ground around them.

"It's time we all went in," Jimi said, putting his empty glass on the railing and turning to go. "Good talk, son. Good talk."

8. A Little Tête-à-Tête

"Hmph. It's you," Rose said derisively as she entered the kitchen.

"Hello," Father Abraham responded, ignoring her tone. "Just washing my hands."

"Only your hands? Why don't you jump in the ocean and be cleansed?"

The storm had arrived with all of the famed intensity of a New England nor'easter, with bone-jarring crashes of thunder, blinding flashes of lightning, and massive waves crashing against the shore.

"I think I'll stick to my hands for now."

"No amount of scrubbing can remove the stain of what you've done," she said caustically.

Abraham paused, hurt by her words. Breathing out, he finished rinsing off the soap and grabbed a towel from the rack. "Let's not argue."

"Oh, no. We wouldn't want that. You're a priest now, and priests never argue. They only condescend."

"I wasn't saying—"

"What exactly were you saying, Abe? That I should keep my mouth shut and go on my merry way as if nothing happened?"

"Of course not."

"It would certainly be easier for you. Be grateful I left. At least you don't have to see me every Sunday."

"Actually, I would like that."

"Spoken like a true man of the cloth."

"Now, Rose. I mean it."

"Yeah, right. You're so practiced, that kind of drivel comes out of you way too easily."

"It's not about what's easy."

"No kidding! Nothing's been easy since that night."

Abe put the towel down in a heap on the counter. "Could we please sit and chat? We can talk things through."

"What's there to talk about? We had an affair while you were engaged to my sister. I had a baby. You took the easy way out by going into the church, and I was forced to give up my child and leave Popplestone. How's that for the whole thing in a nutshell?"

"That isn't fair. At the time, you didn't tell me you were pregnant."

"Fair? Don't talk to me about fair!"

"Please, keep your voice down. We don't want to alarm the others."

"Oh! We wouldn't want to do that!" Rose said, grabbing the towel, folding it, and placing it back on the rack. "Look! I'm still tidying up your messes."

In an attempt to diffuse the situation, he said, "I know it's not my place…"

Rose made to cut him off again, but he persevered.

"…but I'd appreciate it if you'd be willing to sit with me for a moment or two. Please. It won't take long. Let's go to the conservatory where we can be alone."

"You've said that to me before."

"That's not what I meant."

"Watch out. I'm not sweet little Rose anymore."

"Don't I know it," he said under his breath, motioning for her to go first.

"What was that?"

"Watch your step. These stairs can be slippery."

"You act like I haven't been here before."

Abraham followed Rose down stone steps into a circular room surrounded by blueprints and other war-related documentation.

Rose wrinkled her nose. "This doesn't look much like the conservatory. They must have redecorated."

"You're misremembering. This is the Command Center. See the mural and maps? It's not really my thing. The conservatory is above us. Let's go there. It's much cozier."

"Honestly, Abe? Cozier?"

He sighed. She wasn't going to make this easy for him. "After you."

They stepped around a simple wooden pedestal situated in the center of the space and climbed a spiral staircase to the room above. The lightning spilling in from the tall windows made the room look alternately bright and dark. Between the windows, curved shelves lined with dusty books occupied the rest of the wall space. On the other side of the room, a pianoforte sat near a small fireplace, but it looked like it hadn't been played in years.

Rose walked over to it and depressed a key. *Plonk!* "Delightful."

"There's something I need to give you," Abraham said, keeping his voice low and inviting Rose to sit next to him on a velvet-covered loveseat.

She reluctantly sat on the chair beside him. "I don't want anything from you. You've already given—and taken away—enough."

"It's about your mother."

"What does she have to do with anything? She's been gone for years."

"This," he said, producing a letter. When she lifted her hand to take it, he noticed her wedding ring was missing. "Hey, where's your ring?" he asked.

"I used it to make a wish."

"You mean…?"

"Yup. I tossed it into the well."

Abraham looked shocked."

"You were saying?" Rose said, pointing at the envelope.

"Oh, yes. Near the end of your mother's life, she came to confession but didn't say anything. After she left, I found this lying on the seat. I've carried it with me for seven years, waiting for the right moment to give it to you. I'm sorry. It got crumpled along the way, and the envelope's writing has faded. It says, *For Rose, upon the marriage of my first grandchild.*"

"And you never showed this to me?" Rose asked. "How could you?"

"I was bound by her request. I thought you'd understand."

"Give it to me," she said, snatching it from his hands and unceremoniously tearing it open. After squinting at it for a few seconds, she huffed. "I don't have my glasses. You'll have to read it to me."

"Are you sure?"

She glared at him.

"Okay." Abraham took a deep breath and read:

> *To my beloved Rosie,*
>
> *I realize you asked me to keep what I know a secret, but I could not go to my Savior without sharing this with you. After you collapsed, the doctors saved your life by performing a C-section. This much, you know. What you don't know is that after they took out the baby, a beautiful boy, they found a second child. A tiny girl.*

"I had twins," Rose said breathlessly.

"Are you okay?"

The color had drained from her face, and she looked like she was dangerously close to falling over. Abraham reached out a hand to steady her, but she pulled back.

Not knowing what else to do, he said, "There's more. Shall I continue?"

With a determined expression on her face, Rose nodded.

I know it's unlikely that you will ever have the chance to meet them, so I wanted to tell you as much as I remember.

The boy had the cutest face and blond hair. I imagine it didn't stay that way, though. Not being your baby, my sweet Rosie. I gave him a gift. A St. Philomena pendant for good luck. I hope he still has it.

I didn't have a gift for the girl, as we didn't know you were having more than one baby. However, she carried her own gift—a present from God. She has a lovely birthmark on her right arm shaped like angel's wings. I'd never seen anything like it. The doctors hadn't either. They thought it looked like a butterfly, but I know it was a sign. It was a message that your baby would be free to fly in God's light.

You never told me who the father was. I hope you will share this with him as well. He deserves to know.

I love you. Forever.

Mamma

s.d.g.

Rose vibrated with nervous energy. "Abe," she said, her voice shaking. "Toni."

"It can't be," Abraham said, wiping the sweat from his brow. "That isn't possible."

"You just read it. She has the mark. She's got red hair. Toni's our daughter!"

Abraham looked like he was on the verge of throwing up.

"And we had a son, too!" she whispered. "Don't you understand? We had a son!"

A person gasped. It sounded as if they were standing inches away.

"Oh no. There's someone in here with us," Rose said, remembering that the domed ceiling above their heads reflected the slightest sounds from one side of the room to the other. Spinning around, she caught sight of Bianca running down the hall.

Abe tried to get up but fell back down with a thump. "Why was she hiding in here?"

"We have to stop her," Rose said, trying to go after her, but Abraham grabbed her arm. "What? What is it?"

White-faced and sweating, he said, "We have to tell the others."

"That Toni and Marco are cousins? In real life? No way! Knowing that would ruin their lives. No, I'm going to find Bianca and tell her she can't say anything."

"No, you aren't listening. We don't have a choice. We *have* to tell them," he insisted, but Rose pushed him away.

Too dizzy to follow, he watched her run after the bridesmaid.

• • • • •

Bianca didn't know where she was going, only that she had to get out of the conservatory. Over. Up. Down. Around. The castle was a maze, and she was trapped.

A spiral staircase caught her eye, and she went for it. When she reached the second floor, she ran down the hallway, sobbing the entire way, but it was a dead end. Turning around, she frantically peered into every door, searching for a hiding place. Nothing.

Then she noticed the floor-to-ceiling painting hanging on the wall and remembered it concealed a set of hidden stairs to the balcony loft. It was the highlight of every schoolchild's visit to the castle, sneaking behind a painting through a hidden door.

Looking around to see if anyone had followed her, she pulled on the frame, and it swung open. Before her was a narrow, steep, wooden staircase. With one last glance down the hallway, she stepped through and closed the painting behind her.

9. Buyer's Remorse

Bing, bong!

An electronic bell sounded from speakers hidden in every room, followed by Gretta's recorded voice. "King Radimir requests your presence in the castle's great hall. It is time for Magnolia Castle's premiere escape room adventure, *Trapped in a Dungeon*, to begin. Thank you."

Val jerked awake. She was still sitting at the dinner table, surrounded by amaretto cookie crumbs and an empty wineglass.

"If you'd be so kind," Gretta said, appearing beside her. "We're going to clear away the table."

"Of course," Val said, groggily getting out of the folding chair and flopping onto a far more comfortable velvet-lined two-seater against the stone wall.

People appeared from every direction. Maisey joined Frankie and Toni as they emerged from the bridal room. Rose stormed in, followed by Father Abraham. Jimi, Marco, and Christine entered from the patio area where they'd been watching the storm from behind the safety of the castle's tall ocean-side windows, and Tommy slinked over to a chair by the mantle. Turning his back on everyone, he poked at the fire like a kid who'd been scolded by his teacher.

"Let's go, big man," Eddo said, appearing out of the curtains and clapping Tommy on the back.

"All right," he agreed dejectedly, having been denied his surprise game with Bianca. He didn't relish the idea of explaining why he'd never found her.

Father Abraham walked over to Frankie, his shoulders hunched and his expression drawn. "We need to talk."

"After we do the signing thing. Marco, can you come over here?"

"No, now," he insisted.

"Abe, please. Can't it wait five minutes?" Frankie asked.

"It really can't."

"Hey, you look a little peaked. Let's get this over with, so you can have a lie-down."

"You aren't listening to me," Abraham said loudly enough to garner other people's attention.

"Is everything okay?" Christine asked.

"Abe isn't feeling well."

"Let me see," the nurse said, putting the back of her hand on his forehead. "You're burning up. Why don't you sit down for a minute?"

"Not before the kids sign their marriage license," Frankie insisted.

"I'm afraid that isn't going to happen. Maybe later. Nurse's orders. Marco? Can you give me a hand?"

"I must talk with Frankie," Abe said, but Christine and Marco had him by the arms, already leading him to his room.

Toni launched herself out of her chair. "Wait, we're supposed to be leaving."

"Abe will probably feel better in an hour or two. We can sign the papers then," Frankie said. "Right, Val?"

"Right," her sister agreed, even though she wasn't paying attention to the conversation. The scare earlier in the day had taken it out of her, and she hadn't recovered yet.

"Yes, but by then, we'll be locked in," Toni whined. "We aren't supposed to be here."

Father Abraham pulled free of Christine's grip. "Please, my children. Don't argue. I have to speak with—"

He didn't make it two steps before Christine had him again, and this time, she wasn't going to take no for an answer. "Up we go," she said. "Marco, make sure he doesn't trip on those steps."

Toni tried to enlist her mom's help, but Val had no idea what was happening. "What's wrong, sweetheart. Don't you look so beautiful in that dress? I'm so proud of you."

"Oh, Mom, please. They're going to lock us in."

As if on cue, Gretta appeared by her side. "It's time for us to start the game. If you want to leave, you need to go now."

"Can't you wait a little longer before closing the doors?" Toni asked. "We haven't gotten to sign our papers yet. And Marco and I have reservations at the Top of the Harbor Hotel."

"I'm afraid not," Gretta said, checking her watch. "I'm required to close the facility to the public for insurance purposes. Apparently, they have something to say about everything," Gretta added under her breath. It was an uncharacteristic lapse in her facade, which she quickly fixed.

Toni growled in frustration and ran across the room, calling to Marco. He appeared between the stone arches that opened to the second-floor hallway, still helping Christine with Father Abraham.

"I'll be right down," he said with a strained look that spoke volumes.

"Go. It's okay." Christine told him. "I've got it from here."

"Are you sure?" Marco asked, noticing that Abraham had stopped resisting.

"Yeah. I'm good."

"Thanks."

When Marco got back downstairs, he found Toni trailing Gretta around the room, pleading for more time.

"Let's leave," he suggested, catching up to them. "We can sign another time."

"Oh no, you don't!" Frankie said, stomping over. "You can stay with us here tonight."

"What?" Toni blurted.

"You can sign the papers in the morning when Abe is feeling better."

"We have reservations!"

"Look. You don't leave for your honeymoon until next week, so it's no big deal."

"No big deal? It's my wedding night. It's a huge deal!" Toni yelled at the top of her lungs.

"Hey, kiddo," Jimi said, putting his arm around her. "My wedding night didn't work out the way I'd hoped either, but things turned out okay."

"But Uncle Jimi…"

"I know. Hey, don't cry. You don't want to get makeup on that beautiful dress of yours. Chin up. You're a Bellagamba and soon to be an Amato. Nothing keeps us salty New Englanders down. Marco, get over here and act like a husband."

Marco took Toni by the hand, and they sat next to the oversized fireplace, chatting animatedly.

Tommy grabbed the poker he'd been messing with and handed it to Toni. "Here. Poke at the embers. I don't know why, but it helps."

Toni gave him a strange look but took it anyway. Then she jammed it into one of the logs, making a shower of sparks leap out of the fireplace onto the hearth.

"Now that we're assembled—" Gretta said, attempting to get the evening back on track.

"Not quite," Maisey interrupted. "Where's Bianca?"

"She's uh…" Tommy stuttered.

"Indisposed," Rose finished for him. "She'll be down in a minute."

Tommy didn't know what to say, so he kept his mouth shut.

Gretta once more offered for anyone to leave before the game began, making it clear that the windows were barred and the doors would be locked once she left. Toni made a run for it, but Frankie got in her way.

There was another peal of thunder, and the lights flickered. Instantly, everyone's eyes were on Gretta.

"One thousand one. One thousand two. One thousand—" Rose counted aloud.

Jimi looked at the windows. "The storm's getting closer."

"Not to worry," Gretta said. "Should there be a blackout, there are electric candles in every room and emergency guide lights to safe areas."

"Where are the matches?" Rose asked.

"Battery powered. We do not allow open flames inside Magnolia Castle."

"But how do we find them in the dark?"

"Every box is near an emergency night light like this one."

For the first time, everyone noticed the more modern additions to the castle: electric lighting, first aid stations attached to the walls, an AED, and other items scattered here and there.

When everyone finally settled down, Gretta finished her introduction to the game. "The rules are quite simple. Starting with the clue you were given at dinner, you solve a series of puzzles. Each one relates to the castle in some way and will lead you to the next clue. The purpose of the game is not only to have fun but to familiarize yourself with some of the lesser-known spaces."

"Boring," Rose mumbled.

"Yes, Rose," Frankie said. "We all know you are intimately familiar with all of the out-of-the-way places in the castle. I'm sure many a boy enjoyed exploring you...ahem...I mean exploring them with you."

"How droll."

"If you're finished?" Gretta asked, looking pointedly at the sisters.

"By all means, continue," Rose said, staring right back at her before making a show of turning away.

Gretta addressed the people who were paying attention. "Once you solve the last clue, Abraham knows how to end the game. At that time, you will be permitted to leave the castle or, if you are planning to stay overnight, you will be asked to proceed to your rooms.

"Maybe we should have someone other than Father Abraham be the keeper of that knowledge," Christine said, appearing on the steps to the cloister.

"Everything okay up there?" Jimi asked.

"Yeah. He's asleep."

"He must have overdone it again," Rose said, a bit wobbly herself. "You know Abe and drink. It makes perfect sense he chose a profession where he's surrounded by wine all the time."

"That's enough," Frankie said, shushing her sister.

"That may be, but Christine has a point," Jimi said. "Someone needs to check with him."

"I think," Rose stammered, "that considering the circumstances, Gretta should tell everyone where the button is."

"I'll take care of it," Frankie said, shooting Rose a nasty glance.

"But—"

"I said I'll take care of it, and I will."

"All right. All right. Big sis has everything under control, as usual," Rose acquiesced, leaning back and tossing a leg over the chair's arm.

"Then it's time," Gretta announced to the sound of trumpets blaring from the hidden speakers. "King Radimir is counting on you. Good luck. Let the game begin!"

There was a small explosion, a puff of smoke, and Gretta disappeared.

"That's one way to make an exit," Eddo said, pulling out a cigarette.

"You can't smoke in here. It'll set off the fire alarms," Maisey scolded.

"Do I look like I'm lighting it? Sheesh. Touchy, touchy."

Rose looked confused. "Her smoke didn't set off the alarms."

"That smoke wasn't smoke," Tommy explained. "We use it at the hotel for special effects. I think it's mineral oil or something."

Bang! Bang! Bang!

The sound of slamming doors and clanking bolts echoed through the castle.

Tommy spun around, looking in every direction. "I didn't expect that."

Maisey moved closer to him. "Yeah, that was pretty scary."

"Honey, talk to Abe," Jimi suggested to his wife.

"Yeah, I'll do that."

Christine put her finger to her mouth and said, "Shh. Everyone, be quiet. Do you hear that?"

"What's the matter?" Frankie asked.

"I think I hear someone crying."

"I hear it, too," Tommy said. "It must be Bianca."

The banging doors finally woke Val up. "Do you have any idea where she is?"

"No. We were playing a game, but I lost track of her."

Maisey looked concerned. "We'd better find her."

"Everyone pair up and take a different room," Frankie said, motioning with her hands. "The way sound echoes around this place, she could be anywhere."

Rose yawned. "It might be better if she stays hidden."

"What's that?" Val asked, lifting herself off the chair to help with the search.

"Nothing," Rose said, reaching behind her to pour herself another drink.

10. Angel Loft

"Bianca? Bianca? Where are you?" Maisey called, her voice echoing down the long stone hallways like ghosts playing in the shadows. "This place has a lot of steps," she added, emerging from one of the staircases onto the second-floor landing.

Tommy followed close behind. "A lot."

"Bianca?"

"She isn't going to answer you," he said, pausing to listen. "She sounds really upset." Tommy felt strange searching the castle after getting caught in the tower—not to mention the prospect of facing Bianca after not locating her earlier—but he had little choice. It was either this or sit with Rose in the great hall, and that wasn't going to happen. The youngest Bellagamba sister was on a bender that looked like it wouldn't end well for anyone.

Maisey stopped in front of a small alcove containing an immaculate conception statue. "I don't think you're the reason she's crying. It would be more like Bianca to confront you about that kind of thing. Something must have happened."

"That would be great," he said, quickly correcting himself after Maisey glared at him. "No, I mean, I hope I'm not the reason she's upset. But what else could it be?"

"Search me."

Tommy liked the idea of searching Maisey but thought it would be inappropriate to make a joke about that, consider-

ing the circumstances. Instead, he followed her into one of
the guest rooms.

According to the brochures Gretta kept on the lobby
counter, the guest quarters on this side of the cloister weren't
considered in character. They still had stone walls but looked
more like typical hotel rooms, having been prepared for the
castle's less adventurous clientele. The other side of the cloister housed the Wallpaper Room and the King's Suite, re-
splendent with mannequins displaying royal regalia, elaborate
tapestries, and a beautifully carved mahogany bed.

"Why aren't we staying here?" Tommy asked, noting that
the guest quarters looked far more comfortable than the servants' rooms where they were spending the night.

"Frankie wanted us close together instead of spread out
around the castle," Maisey explained, closing the door behind
her.

"Whatever. Have you checked this one yet?" he asked, continuing down the hall.

• • • • •

Frankie led Jimi through a stone passageway beneath the
main castle.

"Can this day get any worse?" he asked.

"Don't jinx it," she said, squeezing through the tunnel.

There was always room for things to get worse when you
lived and worked on the water, like when a boat took a wave
the wrong way or an angler stood too close to the surf. Every
Amato had a healthy respect for the ocean and fate, neither of
which Frankie wanted to tempt.

The castle staff usually kept service entrances like this one
locked, but Frankie and her sisters had spent so much time at
the castle as kids that they knew many of its secrets, including
where the spare keys were kept.

She'd been right when she'd assumed only the castle's
egresses had been barred. Why would they worry about an
interior door that had already been secured? This particular

door led to a workshop situated directly below the lobby. She hadn't been beneath the castle since childhood, and the tunnel seemed much smaller than she remembered. "Ugh."

Jimi stopped moving. "What's wrong? Did you get stuck?"

"No, no. I was thinking about what the cleanup is going to cost."

"Ugh," Jimi agreed.

They took it slowly because the line of service lights, running along a wire strung across the ceiling, looked so old that it might disintegrate at any second. Then they'd really be in a tricky spot.

"Do you honestly think Bianca would come down here?" Jimi asked. "She doesn't seem like the type to enjoy spooky places in the dark."

"I guess not, but people do strange things when they're upset. Their governors get turned off."

"Can't argue with you there. Especially when folks have been drinking."

"Bianca, are you in here?" Frankie asked, pushing through the workshop's decrepit wooden door.

The familiarity of the space instantly came back to her, with its workbenches covered with the marks from countless projects and the musty basement smell punctuated with oil and sawdust. It was one of those places that appeared both well-used and forgotten at the same time.

As if drawn by some inexorable force, she headed across the room to a tall cabinet. Holding her breath, she opened it and screamed.

"What did you expect to find in there?" Jimi said, laughing harder than he had in years. "Her dead body?"

Frankie pushed the old mop that had fallen on her back into the closet and closed the door. "No. It just startled me."

"I'll say! I haven't heard you scream like that since the time a snake got into the old lobster traps."

"I told you never to talk about that!" she snapped, rubbing her arms as if she were cold.

"Listen. Let's go back. Bianca isn't here. And if we're lucky, someone's found her by now."

"Sounds good." With one last glance at the closet, Frankie headed for the door.

• • • • •

Toni collapsed into one of the chairs in the formal dining room. "Charming," she said, squinting at the tortured faces depicted on the medieval tapestry hanging on the far wall.

"We should probably keep moving," Marco suggested, examining the room. "I wonder why we didn't have dinner in here."

Toni crossed her arms defiantly. "Don't know. Don't care. We aren't even supposed to be here. We should be kicking back at the Top of the Harbor Hotel, eating popcorn shrimp, and sipping champagne."

"I know, but everything will be fine. We can sneak into the King's Suite after everyone goes to bed. You can pretend to be my queen, and I'll be your humble but lovable servant," he said, hugging her.

"Pretend? I *am* your queen!"

"True, but do you remember those costumes they have on display in there? I bet you'd look gorgeous *not* in one."

"Stop it. We aren't going to do that with our parents down the hall."

"Okay. We'll find somewhere more private. This place is huge."

"Get your mind out of the gutter," Toni said, pushing herself out of the chair.

"It's my wedding night. It's supposed to be in the gutter."

She slapped him on the arm and chased him into the hall.

• • • • •

Christine made her way to the Wallpaper Room. She'd heard about the secret passageway Toni and Marco had found and thought it might be a smart place to start her search. Lifting the corner of the carpet, she opened the hatch and descended the stairs. However, she was taken aback when she found herself face-to-face with Eddo.

"Oh, it's you!" she said, startled by his presence. "I guess it makes sense that there's more than one way to get in here."

"Yeah," he said, pushing by and climbing out of the tunnel. "She ain't down there."

Christine stared into the darkness, then back at the room above her, and decided it wasn't a good idea to lurk around the castle's hidden places in the middle of the night. She'd leave that to Eddo and the others. So, doubling back, she searched somewhere else.

• • • • •

Val heard Bianca's name being called from every corner of the castle, but she had a hunch the bridesmaid was hiding in the same spot she used to use when she wanted to get away from her sisters.

Whenever the Bellagamba family had visited the castle, they didn't know which areas would be open to the public. Sometimes they could explore the far reaches of the building; other times, things were blocked off. One of their most disappointing visits occurred the day they discovered the tower had been permanently removed from exhibit. No matter how much they whined, no one would tell them why, but rumor had it that someone had died up there.

Truthfully, the tower was the perfect hiding spot, though Val didn't think Bianca had gone there. First, it would have been impossible for anyone to hear her cries because it was supposedly soundproofed, and second, it was way too creepy with that skeleton and swords.

The only plausible location left was the balcony loft—a room situated high above the great hall, cunningly concealed behind arches designed to blend seamlessly with the other decorative embellishments throughout the castle. Local musicians called it the Angel Loft because when choirs sang from there, they sounded heavenly without being seen. Very few visitors got to go up there because it was almost always off exhibit, and most people didn't know about the passage that led to it. They'd stand there staring at the painting, a depiction of Christ feeding the multitude, with no idea of the secret that it hid.

Without a doubt, the Angel Loft provided the most remarkable view of the castle, but Val never went there for that purpose. Being the middle child, she'd spent her life being picked on and left out. And when she was lucky enough to avoid either of those things happening, she struggled to be noticed.

Francesca, the oldest sister, commanded everyone's attention from a young age. She was strong-willed, bossy, and frustratingly right about everything…and Val had never been up to the task of disagreeing with her.

Rosamunda Gabriella Angelina was the youngest and prettiest Bellagamba sister, fawned over by anyone who laid eyes on her. She constantly joked that she could get away with murder simply by batting her eyes. Val had never doubted that for a second.

Valentina, for her part, had always been the empathetic sister, deeply affected by the struggles people faced. To cope with the extra stress, she'd turned to food at a young age for consolation. Whereas Frankie was as hard as Popplestone's rocky shores, and Rose was movie-star thin, Val was soft in every way. She had a gently round face, pillow-like breasts, and cushy arms that had comforted Toni (and countless dogs down at the Ruff Day Rescue) many times over the years.

Exhausted after climbing the cleverly hidden steps to the third floor, Val paused to catch her breath. This high up, the sound of the rain pounding on the cloister's glass roof was deafening. "It's a ripsnorter out there tonight."

Once her heart stopped pounding, she stepped off the landing, and there, just as she'd predicted, was Bianca, scrunched into a ball and sobbing.

Val almost saw herself cowering in the short hallway, but shook off the sensation. "Hi, sweetheart," she said kindly. "Everyone's worried about you. Is there anything I can do to help?"

Bianca looked at her with tears streaming down her face. Her eyes were as wide as saucers, like a terrified wild animal.

"Are you hurt?" Val asked, ambling over and touching her on the shoulder.

Bianca flinched.

"It's okay. Take your time."

The terrified girl tried to speak, but the words came out as broken whispers between sobs. "I…can't…"

"Can't what? Move?"

Bianca shook her head, *No*.

"May I at least tell the others I found you?"

"No!" Bianca gasped, violently shaking her head and grabbing Val's arm.

"Then I'll sit here with you for a minute if that's okay."

"I…have…to…t-tell you something."

"When you're ready."

Bianca shook her head again, but this time it looked more like she was struggling to figure out how to say what she needed to say. "It's…very…bad."

11. Hammer of God

One after another, people returned to the great hall empty-handed. Clearly, Bianca had found an excellent hiding place.

"For the love of God, where's Val?" Frankie asked, having reached the end of her rope. "Don't tell me we've lost her, too."

"Probably fell asleep in a corner," Rose said, slurring her words.

She attempted to get up and stumbled right into Jimi. He caught her and guided her safely back down again.

"Thankths," she said, tipping her glass and spilling amaretto on his shoe.

"Don't mention it."

This time, when the thunder and lightning came, it was directly overhead. The sound was so loud, the rafters shook, and everyone flinched.

Jimi breathed a sigh of relief. "At least the lights didn't go out. I was really worried about—"

As if mocking him, the lights flickered and went dark.

Instantly switching into harbormaster mode, he said, "Nobody move. Give the emergencies time to come on."

Sure enough, the lights above the candle stashes turned on, as well as guide lights that led from every wing of the castle to its great hall.

"I've got a box of candles over here," Christine announced.

With Jimi's help, she handed them out to everyone.

"Wow. They flicker like real candles," Tommy said, turning his on. When he looked up, he gasped. The strange light illuminating everyone's faces from below made it look like he'd stepped into the middle of a horror movie. "I said this place would make a great haunted house. Didn't I? Right when we got in here."

"What are you talking about?" Rose asked, struggling to find the switch on her candle.

Christine turned it on for her and handed it back.

"Well, I never. Isn't that something?"

Frankie's scowl took on a far more sinister appearance in the candlelight. "The real question is, what do we do about finding Bianca and Val? It'll be a lot harder in the dark."

In answer to her question, Val's voice boomed from the balcony. "What?"

"Found her," Rose said, raising her glass in the air.

Jimi leaned back. He could see a faint glow emanating from between the stone arches near the roof. "She's in the loft. I totally forgot about that."

Utterly oblivious to the audience watching from below, Val's round form was silhouetted by a combination of emergency nightlights and bright flashes of lightning above the cloister's glass roof. The effect was terrifying.

Jimi walked toward the stairs. "I'd better go get her."

"I wouldn't if I were you," Rose said, wagging a finger at him

"Why?"

"The Hammer of God is about to descend upon us."

"What does that mean, Rose?" Frankie asked, the dark lines on her face growing more severe.

The youngest Bellagamba sister just smiled. "Give it a second. You'll see."

Val yelled again, her voice booming in between cracks of thunder. "Abraham is Toni's father?"

The shock of what she said stopped everyone's breath in their throats. Reflexively, they turned toward Toni.

"Why is everyone looking at me? That can't be true. It can't be."

Rose held up her finger and said, "As a matter of fact, it is. But that's not all. Wait for the other shoe to fall."

This time, Val's voice rose to a blood-curdling scream. "And Rose is her mother?"

Dropping her finger, Rosamunda Gabriella Angelina added, "That's the one."

Toni gasped and fainted into Marco's arms. Everyone else turned toward Rose. Not even Christine reacted to Toni fainting.

"It's true," Rose said. "I didn't find out myself until Abraham gave me Mamma's note."

"What note?" Frankie asked.

"This note," Rose answered, producing a crumpled piece of paper.

Frankie snatched it from her sister with such force that it tore in two. She only got half, but it was enough to confirm what Val had said.

"Oh my God. It's true. Rose is Toni's mother, but it says nothing about Abe."

"I think I know who planted the seed in my garrrden," Rose said, getting stuck on the *R*.

Frankie grabbed her chest, as if she was having trouble breathing. "How could you do that to Val?" she gasped, throwing herself at her sister.

Rose dropped the wine bottle in her hand, and it crashed to the floor, shattering into a million pieces. The sound of the glass breaking jolted Christine, and she rushed to check on Toni.

"I'll clean that up," Maisey mumbled, going to look for a dustpan.

"But Toni and Marco are almost the same age," Frankie said. "That would mean…"

"It most certainly does," Rose said, taking a wobbly bow. "I had an affair with good ol' Father Abraham while he was engaged to Val. It happened right before your wedding when he broke it off and entered the church."

"You…you…!" Frankie couldn't get the words out.

"Yup, that's me. I'm the witch who casts a spell over every man I meet. Is there any more to drink in this place?"

"I oughta—"

Jimi pulled Frankie off her sister, as Rose cackled hysterically, staggering around the room looking for more wine. "Just like old times, eh?"

"Doesn't that mean they're cousins?" Tommy asked, more to himself than anyone else. "Like, *real* cousins. As in, actually blood related."

This time, everyone looked at Frankie. When she opened her mouth, a sound so animalistic came out that Tommy put his hands over his ears.

Rose laughed again. "And that's not the half of it. And when I say half, I literally mean half."

"What are you saying?" Jimi asked, less controlled than usual. "Why are you hurting your sister and niece like this? I mean, daughter. Good Lord, this is a mess."

"Ready for the kicker, everyone? Hold onto your hats. It's a doozy," Rose said, spinning around like a top about to fall.

Val's voice came from on high one final time. "You have to be kidding me! They had a son, too?"

"Holy moly!" Tommy exclaimed. "Twin cousins!"

"Who is it, Rose?" Frankie asked, getting red in the face. "Tell me right now!"

"That's just it. I never saw the little tike," Rose said with sadness in her eyes. "For all I know, it could be Marco." Then, she laughed again.

That was more than Frankie could take. "Don't even joke about stuff like that!"

"Well, darn," Jimi said, sounding dejected and slumping into a chair.

"What's that supposed to mean?" Frankie asked. "You know that isn't true."

"I don't know anything anymore."

"Oh my God, that's what he meant," Christine blurted.

"Who meant what?" Jimi asked, afraid to hear the answer.

"After Marco left, Father Abraham made me promise not to let his children get married. I didn't understand what he meant. I thought he might be delirious."

"This isn't funny. Rose is *not* Marco's mother. I should know. I'm the one who struggled to push him out for eighteen hours!"

"Of course not," Jimi said, trying to comfort her, "but Abe might be his father. I always knew but didn't want to believe it."

"I never had an affair with your brother. Why would you say that?"

"You'd better have a seat," he said, patting the chair next to him.

Frankie kicked it away. "No, I will not sit down!"

"What's going on, Dad?" Marco asked, bewildered by what his father had said.

"Hold on a minute, son."

"Marco was conceived on our wedding night. That's the whole story, beginning to end," Frankie insisted.

Slumped over and defeated, Jimi retrieved the chair and sat in it himself. "Yes, but that's not the whole story."

"James Amato, don't play games with me or my boy!"

"Maybe we should have this conversation in private."

"Absolutely not. I'm not moving from this spot until you tell me what is going on!"

Jimi took a deep breath and said, "We didn't have…uh… you know…on our wedding night. And then you got sick, remember? We didn't consummate our vows until more than a month later."

"Yes, we did! I remember it plain as day," Frankie insisted.

"Honey, we were drunk out of our minds. I don't think any of us can honestly say we remember anything about that day with absolute certainty."

"I wasn't *that* drunk!"

"Listen to me," Jimi continued. "After the reception, you went to our room to freshen up, remember? And I stayed downstairs in the ballroom because your father wanted a word with me."

"Yes, but you didn't. I was only in there for a couple of minutes before you banged on the door because your key didn't work. I ran out of the bathroom, still washing my face, and let you in."

"That didn't happen," he said, running his hand through his hair.

"Of course, it happened. How else could you have gotten in? You're key didn't work."

"Honey, after I got cornered by your father, it took me at least an hour before I went upstairs to the hotel room."

"Okay. So I lost track of time. What's the big deal?"

"I don't think so. When I got there, Abe ran past me. I figured he was coming from Val's room since hers was next to ours. The thing is, he looked distraught, and I called after him, but he kept running. I shrugged it off at the time. Maybe I shouldn't have because when I pulled out my key, I saw that our door was open."

"Jimi, I don't understand," Frankie said, sitting despite her protestations.

"I closed the door behind me and asked if you were okay. You kind of grunted, turned over, and went to sleep. I assumed you'd had too much to drink—I know I did—and passed out next to you. The next morning, you got sick and spent days in the hospital. By the time you felt better and we...um...anyway, it was a month after the wedding."

"No. I can't believe that's true," she said, putting her head in her hands.

"When we found out about Marco, I knew something didn't add up. You were farther along than you should have been, but I didn't know how to talk to you about it."

"This has to be a sick joke. I remember your red hair. You had a ponytail back then."

"We both did. We thought it was cool because Django had one. You know, from that television show *Django Down Under?*"

"Dad?" Marco asked.

"I'm sorry, son."

Then, everyone noticed something they hadn't before. Jimi had red hair, but it wasn't like Marco's. Jimi's was fair, and Marco's was dark, like Abraham's. Like Toni's.

Marco made like he was going to say something, but then turned and left the room.

"Marco!" Frankie called after him, but Jimi stopped her.

"Let him go. This is a lot to take in. It's a lot for all of us."

Tommy sat up straight, apparently realizing something. "So, wait. They aren't cousins? They're actually half-brother and sister?"

Jimi nodded.

Val's voice came again, but this time she was standing on the steps to the cloister, having found a candle and descended to the hall. No one had noticed that she and Bianca were listening to the conversation.

"So let me get this straight," Val said. "You're telling me that even though I was engaged to that bastard, I'm the only Bellagamba sister he DIDN'T sleep with?"

Filled with rage, her voice howled through the castle as she rushed back upstairs toward Abe's room. When the thuds of her heavy footfalls stopped, a door slammed, and a torrent of muffled swears, screams, and accusations began.

"Should someone go up there?" Maisey asked.

No one responded or moved.

After the ghostly echoes of her voice subsided, Val appeared between the second-floor arches. "I've had a chat with Abraham."

Rose chuckled. "Yeah, we heard. What did he say?"

"He got a bit choked up," Val answered, adjusting her dress. "I'm going to my room for a short rest. When I wake up, I'm going to kill my sisters."

No one breathed again until they heard the door to her room slam shut.

Jimi rubbed his temples. "We need to find out where the panic button is from my brother. I think we've all had enough for one day."

"Not quite," Rose said, stumbling toward the stairs. "It's time Abe and I had a heart-to-heart, too."

"Toni, if you're feeling better," Christine said, "I'm going to check on Bianca."

Still in her wedding dress, Toni grunted and sat lower in her chair.

Frankie burst into tears. "I can't do this right now," and she rushed off.

What was left of the wedding party stood in the candlelight, dumbfounded.

12. Taking Confession

"Knock, knock," Jimi said, standing outside his and Frankie's room.

"Go away," a muffled voice responded. She was lying in the dark on the bed with her newly knitted hat pulled over her face.

"I can't do that," he said, turning the door handle and entering.

Frankie hmphed and turned away.

"I'm sorry that I never said anything. Marco's my son. That's all that mattered to me then, and all that matters to me now."

Frankie peeked from under her hat and scooched over, which Jimi took as an invitation. Closing the door behind him, he approached the bed and lay down next to his wife.

"How can I ever show my face in church again?" she asked through the rows of knitting and purling. "This will be the talk of the town forever."

"We can go to a different church."

"What? Leave the island? To where? Windemere? No way. This is my home. This parish is our home."

"We can ask Abe to put in for a transfer. Priests move around all the time. Perhaps he could visit the Vatican. He's always wanted to explore their archives."

"Father Drummond stayed for thirty-seven years until he was all but mummified," Frankie said flatly.

Jimi couldn't argue with her. "Yeah, that's true."

"To think, I gave confession to your brother year after year, and the entire time, he should have been confessing to me!"

"There's no doubt Abe has much to answer for," Jimi said, watching the dusty blades on the ceiling fan turning slowly overhead. "I honestly don't know what to do."

"He should have told us. He should have told me! He's a priest, for God's sake."

Jimi didn't know how to respond. The only thing he could think to say was, "Maybe we should talk to him."

"Are you crazy?"

"He's my brother. It's not like we can pretend it didn't happen."

"We can try," Frankie said petulantly.

"Listen, he's right down the hall. How about I speak with him first? I have a few things I'd like to clarify, such as the fact that Marco is still *my* son. Nothing can change that."

Frankie pulled the hat up. "I love you."

"You, too," he said, kissing her. "Holy crow! What is that hat made out of? Sandpaper?"

"It's quite warm."

"I'll take your word for it," he said, rubbing his forehead. "I guess it's time to face the music."

"Nope," Frankie said, sitting up. "I'll go first."

"Are you sure?"

Instead of responding, she pulled off the hat and jammed it onto Jimi's head.

"Nice," he moaned, gingerly peeling it back, not wanting to remove a layer of skin with it. "Try to keep things civil, okay?"

She looked at him as if to say, *Really?*

"Okay. Try not to kill him before I get the chance to talk with him."

"I'm not making any promises," she said, grabbing one of the electric candles.

• • • • •

The instant Frankie stepped out of the room, she froze. Far down the hallway, a candle was floating toward her. She almost turned around, but the apparition turned out to be Rose.

"I see you're planning to give the Father a piece of your mind, too," the youngest Bellagamba sister said, squeezing by.

"What did you say to him?" Frankie asked.

"I got my point across," Rose responded and kept going.

As she walked down the corridor, Frankie rehearsed what she wanted to tell Abe, but when she got there, the words died on her lips. "Oh well. I'll have to wing it. I'm not going to bang a uey now."

Assuming Abe knew he was going to get a steady stream of visitors, whether he felt up to it or not, she didn't bother knocking.

The first thing she noticed was the lightning filtering in through a window appropriately shaped like a cross. Technically speaking, it had been designed to mimic an arrowslit, which she knew because she'd spent so much time in the castle. Many an afternoon, she'd pretended to shoot her sisters from that very window. Now, seeing its cross-like shape flicker between darkness and light gave her a chill.

Just to be safe, she genuflected and made the sign of the cross. Then, she pulled a wooden chair over to the side of the bed. It felt hard underneath her, so she grabbed a pillow and sat on it.

Abe was lying on his back, staring at the ceiling, but he didn't acknowledge her. That wasn't surprising. What could he say? Best to lie there and take it. He was a priest, after all. Listening was a big part of his job.

A strange sensation washed over her. In a way, the situation felt familiar, which disturbed her. Clearing her throat, she began.

With the patience of the clergy, Abraham lay there listening as Frankie spoke. She talked about Jimi, how much Marco meant to them, her sisters, and, of course, the fact that the children could never be allowed to sign the license or consummate their marriage. The more she spoke, the more she felt like herself, and the anger inside her began to surface. It didn't take long before she was pacing around the room, flailing her arms and yelling at Abraham.

"Aren't you going to defend yourself? Apologize? Beg for forgiveness?"

When Abraham didn't respond, something broke inside of her. She grabbed the pillow off the chair, jumped on top of him, and pressed it against his face, sobbing as she choked the life out of her brother-in-law. When she finally realized he wasn't moving, she collapsed onto his lifeless body.

Someone knocked on the door.

Wiping the tears from her eyes, she called out, "Just a minute." After a few calming breaths, she rolled off her brother-in-law, stood, straightened her dress, and opened the door.

"Hi, Jimi," she said coolly.

"Is everything okay in there?" he asked, looking over her at Abe in the bed. "Uh, why does my brother have a pillow over his face?"

Frankie turned to follow his gaze. "Oh, that. Because I smothered him."

"You did what?" he asked, pushing past.

Jimi tossed the pillow aside and bent over to check if Abraham was breathing. Then, he checked his brother's pulse. After letting Abe's hand fall to the bed, he looked at Frankie in disbelief. "He's dead."

"I know. I told you. I killed him."

"What's the fuss about?" Rose said, appearing in the doorway. "He deserved to die."

"How do you know?" Jimi asked.

"Because I killed him," she said without a hint of remorse.

"No, you didn't. I did," Frankie corrected.

"Yeah, well, I did it first."

"I hate to spoil your murder party, girls, but I'm the one who killed him. Choked the life right out of him," Val said, poking her head out of her room down the hall and yawning.

"Bull. You couldn't hurt a fly," Frankie said, brushing her off. "You wouldn't even kill ants in the house. You'd have them crawl onto a piece of paper and shake them off outside."

"She's right," Rose agreed. "You're not the type. Besides, I stabbed him with a fillet knife."

"You did what?" Jimi asked, but the Bellagamba sisters ignored him.

"I most certainly *am* the type!" Val continued. "I could murder someone if I wanted to, and, in fact, I did."

"No, you didn't!" Frankie exclaimed. "I smothered him with a pillow."

That's when Jimi lost count of who was yelling at whom.

"If anyone had the right to kill him, it was me."

"No way! I deserved to kill him. Not you two."

"How can you say that after what he did to me?"

"To you? What about what he did to me?"

The sisters' bickering drew the rest of the wedding party into the hallway, and Jimi pushed through, searching for Christine.

"Did Mom kill Uncle Abe?" Marco asked as he passed.

"Possibly. Hang in there, son. I'll figure this out."

Toni was white as a sheet. "Uncle Abe is dead?"

When the rest of the wedding party saw her, they stopped talking.

As if her wedding dress wasn't eye-catching enough, Toni now donned the queen's gown from the King's Suite because her suitcase was safely locked in her car outside the castle. It looked grotesque in the electric candlelight, as if she were wearing a costume for an All Hallows' Eve ball.

Clearing his throat to give him time to think of what to say, Jimi whispered, "I'm afraid he is, sweetheart. You aren't going to pass out again, are you?"

"I don't think so, but I could use a glass of water."

"I'll get it for you," Maisey offered, leading Toni back to her room.

"You aren't kidding, are you?" Tommy asked. "Father Abraham is dead, isn't he?"

The look on everyone's faces told them it wasn't a joke.

"I'm getting the hell out of here!"

"How?" Jimi asked, putting a hand on Tommy's shoulder. "That Gretta woman took our phones, barred the windows, and locked the doors. We're stuck in here until morning."

"What about the panic button?" Tommy asked, searching for a solution.

Jimi perked up. "Right! Frankie? How do we end this thing and open the doors?"

"How should I know?"

"You were supposed to ask Abe about it, remember?"

"Yes, but then we had to find Bianca, and this happened. I have no idea where the panic button is!"

Tommy shook his head. "What a mess."

Back in harbormaster mode, Jimi made a plan. "We need to find that button or anything else that will let us open the doors. Marco, Bianca, Eddo, and Tommy head downstairs to look for it."

"What do you think it looks like?" Tommy asked.

"No idea. Check anything that looks out of the ordinary."

"We're in a castle. Nothing is ordinary."

"You know what I mean."

Eddo broke off from the group and went down the back way.

The sisters made to help with the search, but Jimi stopped them. "Oh, no. Not you three. You need to stay in your rooms until we sort this out."

They protested, but Jimi had plenty of experience with this kind of thing, and he soon had them safely stowed for now. When he returned, he asked Christine if they could have a word.

Ushering her into Abe's room, he said, "I have a big ask. You need to find out which one of them killed him."

"How am I supposed to do that?" she asked, looking extremely uncomfortable.

"You must have gleaned something from those books you read, and being a nurse. You know more about death than any of us."

"I don't make it a habit of hanging around the morgue. I'm more on the saving people side of things."

"Who else can I ask? You're the only person here who won't freak out at the sight of a dead person."

"Not counting you."

"True, but nine times out of ten, mine are floating in the water, and the reason they died is pretty obvious."

Christine shrugged. "Fair point."

"Listen. My wife might have murdered my brother. *My brother*. And if it wasn't her, it was one of her sisters. So could you do me a favor and at least take a look while I deal with the rest of this mess?"

"Of course, Jimi, but you need to find a way out of here before anyone else gets hurt."

"I'm on it."

Noting how easily Jimi slipped into harbormaster mode, Christine said, "I must say, you're awfully calm all things considered."

"If there's one thing I'm good at, it's controlling my emotions during a crisis. What happens after this is over is another matter entirely. I may take up residence in the Windlass for a month or two."

"You and me both. Just as long as they aren't serving amaretto."

"I couldn't agree more. And you don't need me to stay?"

"No. I'm all right."

"Call if you need me. I'll probably be in the great hall."

"Okay," Christine said, closing the door behind him and letting out a sigh. "You were right about one thing, Frankie. I haven't had time to read a thing."

13. Mr. L.

Christine stood in the dark, holding her candle. Its flickering glow made Abraham's corpse look like a monster out of an old horror movie. Moving closer, she put the candle down on the side table.

She remembered him as a virile man, but he now looked gaunt and frail. Death did that to a person. No matter how strong someone may have appeared in life—either physically or because they possessed the kind of charisma that made a crowded room turn to look—death stripped any semblance of strength away.

Not that he deserved to retain any dignity after what he did, Christine thought, and then stopped herself.

It wasn't like her to say things like that, but it had been a long, trying night, and her nerves had worn thin. Usually, she was a positive person. It helped to look on the bright side of things when you were constantly faced with suffering at work.

Her favorite times at the hospital happened when people were wheeled out of their rooms to go home. That would also occur today, but not in a wheelchair. It'd be on a gurney, and Father Abraham wouldn't be headed home. He'd be headed to the morgue.

Looking around, the stark servants' quarters offered little comfort or serenity to lighten her mood. Quite the opposite. They were as barren of life as the priest's body.

Like the narrator in an old noir film, she drawled, "Fate, or some mysterious force, can put a finger on you or me for no good reason at all."

She often quoted lines from her favorite movies and books or spoke with the accent of a favorite character. It was a defense mechanism that helped defuse her anxiety, not to mention her youngest patients thought it was funny. Hearing someone who was suffering laugh or see them smile was worth its weight in gold, as far as she was concerned.

Changing to her normal voice, Christine added, "But this time, I think we know the reason. Quit your dawdling. Time to get to work."

She reached for the light switch but paused. With the power out, her examination would have to be done by candlelight. How fitting for an event titled *Trapped in a Dungeon*.

Slowly, she moved the candle along Abraham's body.

"You really caused a stir, giving Rose that letter," she said, hoping chatting with the deceased priest would help her stay calm. "I never would have thought you'd do something like that."

She'd known Father Abraham most of her life and was pretty torn up about what she'd heard. Even if everything was true, she was convinced there had to be some reason why he'd revealed his secret on this of all days. It seemed malicious, messing with someone's wedding like that, and she'd never thought of him that way. Not once. Something must have forced his hand.

Rose? Possibly. She did seem the type, but she also appeared genuinely shocked by the news that Toni was her daughter. And when she made that quip about Marco being Abraham's son, it sounded like a joke, not that she actually knew it to be true.

Frankie? Val? Did they know?

Not a chance. There's no way any of them would have allowed the wedding to proceed if they'd known Toni and Marco were blood relations, which brought her back to the question of: *why?* Why did Abraham do it? Why did he let things get this far only to air out his dirty laundry now? Maybe the answer was in the letter. She should examine it at some point.

Christine stared at Abraham for a long while and then scolded herself for procrastinating again.

"Okay, get on with it. You've read enough murder mysteries to know what to do. Put yourself in Ms. Prissy Langenshire's shoes."

First introduced to the small village of Barton-Marsely's famed amateur sleuth on British TV, Ms. Prissy Langenshire's books had been Christine's constant companion when on break, lounging poolside, or when she should have been doing *more important* things. Ms. L. was a funny lady with a big laugh that set her English neighbor's teeth on edge, but she always figured out who committed the murder, much to the chagrin of the local constabulary.

"Think, think, think," Christine told herself. "If Frankie used a pillow to smother him, there should be fibers in his airway. I need some tools."

She checked the drawer in the bedside table and found a Bible.

"Unfortunately, you aren't going to be much help, Gideon. Father knew the verses in that book of yours by heart, not that it did him any good. I can think of several he should have considered before jumping into bed with his brother's wife *and* her sister."

Closing the drawer, she moved to the other side of the room, where a roll-top desk waited in the corner. When she opened it, she saw a pad with the words *Notes from Magnolia Castle* across the top next to a line drawing of the building's famous facade. Beside it was a golden pen and a postcard.

"Gretta thinks of everything," she said, rerolling the top.

Next, she rummaged through the desk's drawers. That proved to be more fruitful.

Holding up a reading magnifying glass and a flashlight, she said, "I doubt either of you were left here for this purpose, but we use what we've got. Now for the hard part."

Reaching into her pocket, she pulled out a pair of blue, non-latex gloves. Carrying them around had become a habit working in a hospital, and they'd come in handy more than once. She was particularly glad she had them today.

Gently pushing on Father Abraham's chin to open his mouth, she peered inside. Christine saw several metal fillings but no fibers. She also noticed that his skin had a pink tint, which surprised her. Ms. L. always expected people who'd been suffocated to have burst blood vessels in their eyes or blue lips, but that wasn't the case.

"I'm no expert, but I don't think Frankie did it. Jimi will be glad to hear that."

Christine sat back to plan her next inspection. Working backwards, she focused on Rose.

"How did she say she killed him? Stabbed him, right? But where? There isn't any blood. Sorry about this, Father, but I need a look at your back."

Grunting with the exertion, she pushed Abraham onto his side.

"Rose wasn't lying. How in the world did she stab him from behind? Oh. He must have been standing or lying like this, listening to her, I guess. But wait…"

In the center of his back, there was a small incision surrounded by a dark red stain. There was also blood on the bed's white sheets, but nowhere near as much as she'd expected. The bed would have been saturated if he'd been alive when he was stabbed. Having seen everything she needed, Christine let Abraham lie back down.

"Rose didn't kill you. She stabbed you after you were already dead. It's looking more and more like you were telling the truth, Val. I never would have guessed you had it in you. Okay, last check."

As politely as possible, she removed Abraham's collar and unbuttoned his shirt to look at his throat.

"Huh. This is getting weirder by the second. No bruising, and your hyoid bone isn't broken. That's a relief. But—"

She stood up quickly.

"Holy cow! None of them killed you! Pardon me, Father, but you were already dead when Val strangled you, too. That's why there aren't any marks. You were already dead!"

Remembering Abraham wasn't feeling well when she and Marco had helped him upstairs, she took a step back from the body.

"You weren't just upset. You were sick. Dying even. I hope it wasn't anything catching."

She put one arm over her mouth and nose and made the sign of the cross with the other.

"Calm down, Christine. Few things can make you get sick and die that quickly. If his death *was* related to an illness, it's far more likely that he died from a preexisting condition. Possibly a heart attack or stroke."

Regaining her composure, she tried to reason things through. "Ms. Langenshire, don't fail me now. What would you do in a situation like this?"

Doing her best impression of an English accent (which wasn't very good, but Abraham didn't object), Christine said, "And so, we come to the thing of it. We must see if there are any outward signs of a struggle."

"Struggle, right!" Christine exclaimed, returning to her normal voice. "Thanks, Ms. L."

Carefully lifting Abraham's arm by the sleeve, she inspected the priest's fingers.

"What's that?" she asked, getting a whiff of a pungent odor. "Did you spill something on your hands?"

She leaned closer.

"Ah. Been drinking the cocktails, I see. Whoever heard of an almond-themed event anyway? Weddings can make people do the strangest things."

She dropped the arm and wiped her hands on the bedspread for good measure.

"It's not as dramatic as *skin under the fingernails*, but it's a start. Let's find out what you were drinking. Maybe that will lead me to who you were talking to."

But before she left, she knelt to pray for Father Abraham.

Just as she said, "Amen," the lights came back on.

"Should I take that as a sign?" she asked herself. "Absolutely. Thanks, Abe."

Flipping the switch to turn off her electric candle, she headed downstairs to continue her investigation.

14. Amaretto Cocktails

"Did you figure out who did it?" Jimi asked when Christine appeared in the great hall, where everyone remained gathered.

"No," she answered, obviously preoccupied.

"It was worth a shot."

"No, I mean, none of them did it."

"Oh. Abe died of natural causes?"

"That's not what I'm saying, either."

"Enough of this dance, Christine. What *are* you saying?"

"I'm sorry, Jimi. I don't mean to be evasive. It's a lot to process, and I'm not there yet. Give me a second."

She pushed past him and motioned for everyone to gather around.

"What's up, Auntie Christine?" Toni asked, hiking up her queenly dress.

"Does anybody know what Abe had to drink?"

"Wait a second. Are you saying he was poisoned?" Jimi whispered.

"Not necessarily. I smelled something on his hands, and I'm trying to figure out what it was."

"Like gasoline?" Tommy asked.

Bianca slapped his arm. "She said *drink*, you nimrod. Why would he be drinking that?"

"How should I know? She said she smelled something on his hands. I hate when I get gas on my hands. It's so hard to get off."

Bianca rolled her eyes.

"What?"

"Quiet down, you two," Jimi said, shutting down their little spat. "I asked Christine to figure out what happened. Please, let her do her job, even if we don't understand what she's getting at."

"I think it was a cocktail," Christine clarified.

Maisey lifted an empty bottle off the table and said, "It's not as if we can do a process of elimination or anything. There are too many empties lying around."

"Why don't you have Marco mix some of the drinks?" Jimi suggested. "Then, you can see if they smell like what you're looking for."

Christine nodded. "That's a good plan."

Jimi elbowed Marco in the side. "Told you that job at *Joanie's Wayside Watering Hole* would come in handy someday."

The nurse handed Marco a pair of blue gloves.

"What are these for?" he asked.

"Humor me," she said, patting him on the arm.

Together, Christine and Marco organized what remained of the alcohol and mixers.

"One of you will have to tell me what people were having," Marco said, inspecting a bottle to see how much amaretto was left.

Jimi pointed upstairs. "Your mother knows. She's the one who set everything up."

"Want me to check with her?" Marco asked.

"I guess."

"You don't have to. I know," Toni said, stepping over to the table. "She showed the catering list to me. Let's see. There was an Italian Margarita—"

Tommy perked up. "I liked that one."

Bianca kicked him in the leg and put her finger to her mouth.

"Toasted Kahlua Cocktail, and Amaretto Coffee—"

Christine made a face. "I think we can rule those out. I would have smelled the coffee."

Toni continued. "Amaretto Sour—"

"That one's a possibility," Christine interrupted again, making a note in a small book she'd pulled out of her pocket.

"Amaretto On The Rocks, and Amaretto 'Bama Slammer."

"I never knew there were so many different amaretto drinks," Maisey said.

"Line 'em up," Jimi told his son.

Marco looked at Christine. "Any particular order?"

She shook her head. "Nope."

"And you don't want me to make the coffee drinks, right?"

It took a moment for the nurse turned detective to respond as she thought about it. "Actually, make them anyway. It can't hurt."

Marco nodded and got to work. When finished, he placed six glasses on the table. "I wouldn't drink the coffee one," he said, pointing to the first glass. "I had to grab an old cup off the mantle to make it."

Bianca stuck out her tongue. "Nasty."

Maisey yawned. "I could use a coffee right about now. I can't keep my eyes open."

"I'm not planning on drinking any of them," Christine explained. "I only want to smell them."

Everyone watched her intently as she methodically made her way down the line—choosing a glass, walking away from the table, and sniffing it. "Definitely not either of those. And this one's too fruity. It was similar to this one, but not quite the same. It's not burnt enough."

"Burnt?" Jimi asked. "Like toasted almonds?"

"No, more like almonds that have turned. Almost bitter." When the word came out of her mouth, she froze. "Bitter almonds. Bitter almonds. What does Ms. Langenshire always say?"

"Who's that?" Tommy asked.

Bianca harrumphed. "I can't believe you don't know who Ms. Prissy Langenshire is. Haven't you ever read a book?"

"Yeah. I've got lots of graphic novels."

"That doesn't count!"

"Of course, it counts."

"Shh! Be quiet for a minute," Maisey said, silencing them.

For a long while, the only sound in the great hall was the rain pattering on the windows as Christine slowly turned in circles in the middle of the room.

When she spoke, she adopted an English accent. "Some consider poison to be a cowardly way to kill, but I disagree. Anyone can grab a hammer and do the deed in a fit of rage, but it takes a cold and calculating mind to poison a person. You see, not all poisons are the same. One may choose strychnine, for instance, a particularly hideous way to die. It might take two to three hours to take effect, making it a good choice for someone trying to escape. But, most murderers want to see the result of their plans, so quick is more to their liking. That's where cyanide comes in. Fascinatingly, it leaves a telltale sign detectable by only about half the population. Those who can, say it smells like bitter almonds…bitter almonds…"

Switching to her normal voice, Christine yelled, "Oh, no! Abraham *was* poisoned!"

"In his drink?" Bianca asked. "Then everyone might have been poisoned!"

Tommy grabbed his head and moaned. "We're all going to die."

Maisey slapped him hard in the face. "That's not helping. None of us wants to die."

"I feel like a punching bag. Anyone else want to take a swipe?" Tommy asked, massaging his cheek.

"Jimi, go check on your wife and her sisters," Christine said urgently. "Make sure they're okay. Everyone else, stay right here and don't move."

Bianca waved her hands nervously in the air. "I can't stand around waiting to die. I wish Father Abraham were here."

"Why?" Toni asked.

"You know. So we can confess."

"I pissed in the trophy cup!" Tommy blurted.

Maisey spun around. "What are you on about?"

"Just what I said. I pissed in the trophy cup. Remember when the girls' cross-country team won the state championship our senior year?" he said, pacing back and forth.

"Uh, huh."

"We got drunk, and Jake dared me to take a leak in the trophy because it looked like a giant cup, and I did."

"No wonder it stunk!" Bianca said. "That is totally gross."

"Why are you telling us this now?" Maisey asked. "Who cares about an old cross-country trophy?"

"I couldn't die without telling Bianca. I remembered she was the one who had to clean it, and I was so embarrassed. I'm sorry, Bianca. It was stupid."

Maisey's laugh had a hysterical twinge to it. "Dude, you are *so* Catholic."

Toni stood up and announced, "This is perfect. I'm going to die on my wedding day wearing a ratty old costume."

"I'm pretty sure you don't have anything to worry about," Christine said, attempting to calm everyone down. "We'd be dead already if our drinks had been poisoned."

Tommy pushed the nearest glass away and said, "That may be, but I'm not touching another drop."

"That's a good idea. No one should," Christine agreed. "Stick with closed containers: water bottles, sodas, and stuff like that. For those who don't know, there's a vending machine on the other side of those curtains."

"Was everyone okay up there?" Bianca asked when she saw Jimi come down the steps.

"No one's dead. Wait, that didn't come out right. My brother's still dead, of course, and they didn't take the news of the poison very well, but that's no surprise."

Christine placed a hand on her forehead. "I need a quiet place to figure this out. I think it's a good idea if I talk to people individually to make sure everyone's stories line up."

"I thought you said you weren't good at this detective stuff?" Jimi asked.

"I'm getting the hang of it. Like you, I work best under pressure."

"How about the bridal room?" Maisey suggested.

Christine shook her head. "I don't think so. Somewhere no one can hear us."

"Good luck with that. This place is an echo chamber," Tommy said loudly enough that his voice bounced off the walls.

Rose appeared in the entrance from the cloister. "There's one place that isn't like that."

Jimi spun around. "Hey, you three were supposed to stay in your rooms."

"Not going to happen, honey," Frankie said, leading her sisters down the stairs. "And Rose is right. There's one place in this castle that's soundproof. The tower."

"That's off limits," Tommy said, scuffing the floor with his foot. "I should know."

Val pointed to her sisters. "True, but we know how to get in. They keep a spare key in a hidey-hole in the wall. Come on. I'll show you."

Everyone followed the Bellagamba sisters across the great hall and through the red velvet curtains at the other end.

With a mischievous look, Val reached into a hole in the wall and retrieved an old metal box. "See? We found it ages ago when we used to come here."

Jimi looked skeptical. "I imagine they've changed the lock since then."

"Oh, Jimi-boy, have a little faith," Rose said, leaning on the harbormaster. "Nothing changes on the Cape. You know that. Besides, this is a museum. They're obsessed with keeping everything the same."

Val opened the box, lifted a keychain with two keys on it, and gave it to her younger sister.

"Drumroll, please," Rose said before using the bigger of the keys to unlock the heavy steel door.

Bianca cringed, expecting it to screech as all dungeon doors should, but it swung open without a sound.

Then Rose used the smaller key to open the padlock holding the barred door shut. "All set," she said as the chain slid to the floor with a clang.

Christine stepped forward. "I'm going up. No one follows me until I call for you. Got it?"

Everyone nodded their heads.

"We'll wait in the hall until you're ready," Jimi said, ushering everyone back through the curtains.

15. The Tower

Christine installed herself in the armory, surrounded by countless instruments of death. The irony wasn't lost on her, but hanging out in the first-level dungeon was too morbid, considering the circumstances. That being said, the cell might come in handy if she figured out who murdered Father Abraham. But that was a big *if*. Right now, she needed to review the facts and look for a pattern.

"Look at me. I'm thinking like a detective," Christine told the suits of armor standing at the ready by her sides. "Ms. L. would be so proud!"

Proud, maybe, but Christine was still stuck because although the two pieces of the letter, plus the subsequent revelations about Marco and Toni's parentage, certainly put Frankie, Rose, and Val in the frame, all three Bellagamba sisters seemed genuinely surprised at the news. And why would they kill the priest twice? To shift the blame away from themselves? Possibly, but she'd never known a Bellagamba to hide their feelings. No, they probably weren't the culprits.

"There I go again! *Culprit* is such a cool word. Okay, what is it that Ms. L says?

Clearing her throat, Christine spoke in a British accent, "Start at the beginning and go through it step by step. There are always clues hidden along the way that may not mean anything at the time but make sense when you link them together."

"You're so smart, Ms. L!" she said, returning to her normal voice. "The problem is, I arrived late. Therefore, the only way to piece together what happened earlier in the day is to speak to people."

As if in response to her plan, a knock echoed up the tower's spiral stairs.

"Yes?" she asked, irritated that whoever it was hadn't waited for her.

Bianca's meek voice echoed from below. "Can we come up?"

"I thought everyone agreed to wait until I called for you."

The bridesmaid was silent for a few seconds before responding. "Yes, but we need to speak with you right away."

"Who's we?"

"Me, Maisey, and Tommy."

"Are you trying to ambush me?" Christine asked, searching for a weapon that would be a good choice for defending herself from an attack by three half-drunk young adults in wedding attire. "I'm warning you. I have a sword in here."

Tommy's concerned voice wafted up like a specter at midnight. "She isn't kidding. I saw it when I was up there earlier."

"What do you mean, *when you were up there?*" Bianca interrupted.

"Um, you know. Before," he said sheepishly.

Bianca sounded quite put out. "How *before?*"

Maisey, who was growing increasingly uncomfortable wearing the skimpy bridesmaid dress she'd chosen, not to mention the murder investigation, lost all patience with their constant banter. "Get a room, you two. Then you can argue as long as you want."

"I'm waiting," Christine said.

This time, the pause was longer. Then all three spoke at once. "Please, let us come up."

"Okay. One by one. And no funny business."

Bianca appeared first, with her hands in the air. "Uh, guys? Tommy was right. She *does* have a sword."

Christine used it to point to a chair she'd set out for interrogation purposes. "You can put your hands down."

Bianca hesitantly lowered her arms and sat down, never taking her eyes off the weapon.

Next, Maisey walked into the room, and Christine motioned for her to sit on the floor next to Bianca. Several seconds passed, but Tommy didn't show.

"Is he coming?" she asked.

"I'm here," he said, poking his head around the corner. "I was waiting to make sure it was safe."

"Sit down, you foolish boy."

Tommy lowered himself to the floor next to Maisey, and she nudged him with her elbow.

"Ow. Okay. I'll tell her." Taking a deep breath, he said, "Listen, Christine, we didn't do it."

Bianca nodded her head vigorously. "None of us killed anybody. Honest."

Christine picked up the shield Tommy had been playing with earlier that day with one hand and planted the sword in the floor next to her with the other. "Silence!"

She looked formidable, flanked by the suits of armor and sitting on King Radimir's throne.

Leaning forward, she said, "I saw you talking to Father Abraham when I entered the castle. You were huddling with him in the room at the bottom of the stairs, near the great hall. What were you talking about?"

Instantly, the room was filled with protestations, but when Christine pointed the sword in their direction, they quieted down.

"I want you to tell me what you were talking about," she insisted, "and don't leave anything out."

"Do we have to?" Tommy asked.

Maisey had a strained look on her face, which clearly showed that she didn't want to talk about it. "It didn't have anything to do with this."

"I'll be the judge of that," Christine said, looking rather regal in the velvet-covered chair with her sword and shield.

Tommy shook his head. "I'm not telling her."

"Why not?" Maisey asked. "You were the reason for it."

"Hey, I didn't do anything."

"Men always say that."

Looking thoroughly embarrassed, Bianca did her best to explain. "Father Abraham gave us the talk."

"The talk?" Christine asked.

Tommy cringed. "Don't make her say it."

Christine didn't look away, and Bianca gave in. "Um…Like when a man and a woman love each other…"

"Aren't you three a little old for that?"

"He also gave me these," Tommy said, sheepishly producing a handful of condoms. "He said he knew boys would be boys, but those same boys should at least be considerate of the girls."

Christine laughed so hard she almost dropped the shield. "That has to be the most ridiculous alibi I've ever heard."

Bianca, Maisey, and Tommy sat there with blank expressions on their faces. They didn't appear to find it funny in the least.

It took a while for Christine to catch her breath. When she did, she asked. "What did you do after that?"

"Stayed as far away from Father Abraham as we could!" Tommy said resolutely. "I, for one, wasn't going to risk another conversation like that."

"What about the rest of you?"

"Same," Bianca said. "One lecture was enough for one day."

Maisey nodded in agreement. "Me, too."

Christine chuckled. "Well, no one ever told Ms. Langenshire anything like that."

"You enjoy those books, don't you?" Tommy asked.

"Yes, I do. You should read one. You might learn something."

"He reads books that have more pictures than words," Bianca said with a sour expression on her face.

"Picture books?"

"No, comics," Bianca explained.

"Graphic novels, thank you very much," Tommy corrected.

Christine leaned the shield beside the chair. "Okay. Let's say, for the time being, that I believe you. That would mean none of you knew about Toni or Marco, right?"

What little color Bianca's face had gotten back instantly disappeared again. "No way! Not in a million years. I never thought that."

"Why not? The resemblance is striking if you think about it. Same color hair, similar facial structures. If you know what to look for, it's pretty obvious, I would say now that the cat's out of the bag."

Bianca held herself as if she were cold. "I assumed that kind of thing was what attracted them to each other. But I never thought they were related. They aren't the only redheads in this town. Not by a long shot."

"And what about you two?" Christine asked.

Tommy shook his head slowly. "I mean, they used to sneak under the bleachers. If I'd suspected anything like this, I would have mentioned it."

"Or made a joke about it," Bianca said. "He makes jokes about everything."

"Not this! It gives me the heebie-jeebies!"

"Imagine if you were Toni," Maisey said. "She must be suffering right now."

Tommy threw up his hands. "And I imagine pretty glad she made the pledge thing to save herself until she got married, or this would be a lot worse. She's still wearing that ring, isn't she?"

Maisey gave him a withering look. "Of course she is. She wouldn't take it off now."

Christine sat patiently while they talked. Their responses appeared sincere, and she relaxed. "I've known you all for many years, and I've never taken any of you for liars. So, I'm inclined to believe you, but this doesn't mean you're off the hook. Understand?"

All three nodded.

"Good. Let's move on. Who else did you see talking to Abraham?"

"Lots of people. He's everybody's priest," Tommy said. "There must have been a hundred people here."

"I don't mean, 'Hi, how are you?' I mean, *really* talking to him. The kind of conversation where he might have said something that set another person off. Focus on the wedding party."

Maisey remembered something. "He walked down to the rocks with his brother."

Tommy piped up. "Oh yeah! After Toni and Marco disappeared from the room, Frankie had to call for him. You know about that, right?"

"Yes. Toni told me earlier. I guess that means I need to talk to Jimi next," Christine said, tapping her notebook.

Bianca inched closer. "Can we stay? I don't like it down there."

Christine considered this and said they could remain, provided they didn't interrupt. "No funny business. Do you understand? I ask the questions."

Bianca mouthed, *Thank you.*

"No problem," Tommy said, hopping to his feet. "Where do you want us?"

"You, my friend," Christine instructed, "are going to fetch Jimi while we girls get things ready."

"Aw," he said, scuffing his foot on the ground.

Christine waved her hand at him and said, "Get a move on, Tommy-boy. Okay, girls. Let's get down to business."

16 · James Amato

When Tommy returned with Jimi, they were surprised to find Christine sitting on the throne with Maisey on one side holding the sword and Bianca on the other holding the shield.

"Whoa," Jimi said, sitting in a chair obviously meant for him. "Aren't you taking this a little far?"

Tommy remained behind Jimi, not wanting to get in the way.

"You may have asked me to do this job, but I get to decide how I do it," Christine said.

"Whatever you say, Your Majesty." Jimi made a slight bow of his head. "What do you want to know?"

"You talked with your brother on the rocks, correct?"

"Yup."

"What did you speak about?"

"Nothin'."

"Jimi, if this is going to work, you'll have to be more helpful than that."

"Abe waxed rhapsodic about the lighthouse or some fool thing and said I should be proud of Marco. I said I was, and then Gretta, that serious lady from the front desk, told me I needed to go in."

"Yes, we all know who Gretta is. And you went right in?"

"No. Not right away. We talked about our jobs a little, and that's when Frankie called. I know better than to ignore her, so I got a move on. I might have handed him my drink before

I left, too. Yeah, that's right. Then I walked to the castle, and Frankie brought me to the Wallpaper Room on the second floor. I'm sure you've heard about Toni and Marco arguing and how their moms locked them in there to work things out. That didn't go so well. They snuck out using a secret passageway and nearly gave Val a heart attack. I guess Frankie should have seen that coming. We're in a castle, after all."

"Yes, I heard about that, and I've seen the secret hatch," Christine said, making notes in her book. "Did you see Abraham after that?"

"Sure, at the wedding, if you can call it that. Never been to anything like it. I mean, the cake was on the ground."

"No, I don't mean in front of everyone. Alone, with just the two of you."

"Nope."

"Are you sure?" she asked, pressing the harbormaster.

Maisey and Bianca followed her lead, scrutinizing his expression, but Jimi was as worn as a piece of driftwood.

"Sorry. I didn't see him except when everyone else was around at the wedding, in the pictures, and at dinner before he went upstairs. I've been thinking about that."

"Oh?"

"I thought he looked pretty upset at the time, but now I think he looked sick."

"Yes, that was my conclusion, too. He was already feeling the effects of the poison."

"Weird."

Christine finished writing in her book. "I guess that's all for now. I'll speak with Toni and Marco next."

"You can't think—"

"Next," she insisted.

"Yeah, yeah. You're the boss. Are you sure that's all you want to know?" he asked, getting ready to leave.

"One last question. What did your brother do with the drink you handed him?"

"I think he put it on one of those tables the caterers left out. He's more of a rocks guy. Doesn't...I mean...he didn't go in for mixed drinks."

Jimi looked sad.

Christine felt bad for grilling him at such a difficult time. "I'm sorry for your loss, Jimi. I'm just trying to be thorough."

"I know my brother had his faults, but Abe was a good guy. He did right by the people at his church, and many will miss him. Me included."

Christine smiled kindly at him. "We'll figure this out. I promise."

Jimi nodded and left. His footfalls sounded heavy as he descended the tower, followed by Tommy, who'd been direct-ed to retrieve Marco and Toni.

While they waited for the next set of interviewees, the girls chatted about what Jimi had said.

Interrogating everyone didn't seem as fun anymore, seeing how sad Jimi was. Even so, they didn't completely shut the door on his involvement because if it wasn't them, and it wasn't Jimi, Frankie, Val, or Rose, they were running out of suspects.

• • • • •

"Does Christine honestly believe I killed my brother?" Jimi asked Tommy as they passed the dungeon with the skeleton.

"Beats me. I mean, who kills a priest at a wedding? It's the kind of thing that happens in a movie, not real life."

"No kidding," Jimi agreed as Tommy skipped past him to get Marco and Toni.

Left alone in the dim light, Jimi studied the dungeon dis-play. There was a rotting cot with a skeleton draped across it, with several fake rats on the stone floor. To one side, a broken lantern flickered with fake candlelight, and a wooden display stand held an actual, human skull—broken, as if it had been smashed by something hard. Unlike the bleached-white fake skeleton, it looked old and weathered.

"Unknown sailor. Served aboard the Mayflower," Jimi said, reading the brass plaque. "I wonder if it's real. In fact, I wonder about a lot of things, like, *What were you thinking, Abe?* If you'd looked at that note, we wouldn't be in this mess, and you'd still be alive. But that was you, always playing by the book...and playing the field. What a mess. I really needed this like a hole in the head. Oh, sorry. I didn't mean it like that. Just a figure of speech," he said to the human skull that actually had a hole in it. "But I really do wish you were still here, little brother. Things won't be the same without you."

17. Well Wishing

Tommy returned to find Christine alone in the armory. Before he could ask where Maisey and Bianca were, she told him to wait in the chapel on the third level. He was disappointed that he wouldn't have the opportunity to hear Toni and Marco's side of the story, but left without making a fuss.

It was the second time he'd climbed the stairs to the tower's top level that night. Only this time, he found his friends sitting cross-legged on the floor, waiting for him.

"This is a disaster," he said, sitting beside Bianca.

She leaned her head on his shoulder and sighed. "No kidding."

"I'm sorry I didn't find you earlier."

"Yeah, me, too."

"Huh," Maisey said to herself.

Tommy and Bianca turned to see if she was trying to get their attention.

When she didn't respond, Tommy asked, "And?"

"Oh. I was wondering why Jimi asked Christine to investigate. I know she's a nurse, but don't you think he's ignoring something important?"

"What?" Bianca asked, yawning and stretching her arms.

"What if she's the killer?"

That woke Bianca up. "No way!"

"Shh. Keep your voice down," Maisey said, looking around. "She might hear us."

"I don't think she can. This tower is strange that way," Tommy whispered, not taking any chances.

Bianca insisted that Christine couldn't be the murderer.

"Why not?" Maisey asked.

"She's nice! She'd never do anything like that. And she's a nurse! Nurses don't go around killing people."

"I heard of one that did," Tommy said.

Bianca punched him on the knee.

"What'd you do that for? It's not me who goes in for that gruesome stuff. Christine's the one who reads murder mysteries. I like sports."

"So, let me get this straight," Bianca said. "You're saying that she's the murderer because she reads books? That makes as much sense as saying you read about sports, so you must be a sports star."

Tommy looked perplexed for a moment and then said, "Oh."

"All I'm saying is we need to keep an open mind," Maisey explained. "What better cover than to be the investigator?"

Bianca gave her a funny look. "Now, you're sounding like those mysteries Christine reads, where it's always the person you least expect, no matter how outlandish it might seem."

"True, but in this case, it very well might be her."

Tommy scratched his head. "Yeah, I don't think so."

"Me neither," Bianca mumbled.

"I don't see either of you offering a better alternative."

"I know one thing," Tommy said, rubbing his weary eyes. "I'm not going to be able to sleep after this."

"Me neither," Bianca agreed, curling up next to him and laying her head on Tommy's lap.

Maisey rested her head on her knees. "None of us will. At least not comfortably."

"And I'm never—" Bianca paused to yawn. "—ever setting foot in this castle again."

• • • • •

In the armory, Christine thought about her list of suspects as she grabbed a second chair for Marco.

"You're punching above your weight class," she said aloud.

"What's that?" Toni asked, appearing in the doorway.

"Oh, nothing. Toni, please sit there. This one's for you, Marco."

"Sure," he said, hesitantly sitting beside his former fiancée.

Christine noticed that Toni, who was still wearing the queen's garments from the King's Suite, angled her chair away from him. That's when she realized she should have asked them to come separately. She couldn't imagine what they were going through. And what if they—

"Don't worry," Toni said, cutting off her thoughts.

"What? I mean, worry about what?"

Toni tilted her head knowingly. "I could tell by the look on your face what you were thinking."

"Sorry. Was it that obvious?"

"Yeah, and it will be for everyone who looks at us from now on," Toni said with an edge to her voice Christine had never heard before. "Once this is over, I'm ripping the rearview mirror off my car and never looking back."

Her words hurt Marco, but what could he say? It's not like they had a future. Besides, Toni was right. By tomorrow, all of Popplestone would be talking about them.

Any way you looked at it, the two of them would never be free of this, at least not on the island.

Popplestone was separated from the mainland by a long and winding saltwater river. The highway crossed it on one side and the Split Bridge on the other. The latter used to be the only way to and from the harbor's rocky shores until the state built the tall bridge near the quarry. Now, the Split mainly served as a smog generator, backing up lines of cars as boats on the river emptied into the harbor. It was one of the island's most cherished and disdained landmarks by tourists and locals alike, serving as an apt metaphor for the people who lived there—simultaneously connected *and* cut off from the mainland at the same time.

Now Toni and Marco would be separated from their community not by distance but by the stigma of having been in a long-term relationship. How sad that love could create such a negative situation for them, especially considering they'd had no idea they were half-siblings until Val had shouted from the rafters.

"I'm sorry I made you climb up here wearing that," Christine said to Toni. "Please be careful going back down."

"I will. I'm kind of getting used to it."

Obviously wanting to get the interview over and done with, Marco asked, "What do you want to know?"

Taking the cue, Christine said, "I need you to explain what happened in the Wallpaper Room."

Toni and Marco made eye contact for the first time since entering the room. She'd struck a nerve.

"I won't tell anyone," she assured them, "unless it concerns Abe's murder."

"It doesn't," Marco said flatly.

Toni shook her head.

Christine was relieved. "Then you won't have any trouble telling me."

"And you promise not to say anything?" Marco asked.

"As much as I can."

"Mom would be pissed if she found out."

"Mom...I mean, Val...would be, too," Toni added.

"Oh, Toni," Christine said softly. "Val is still your mom. She'll always be your mom. I've never known anyone who loved their child more than Val."

Toni smiled weakly.

"Just tell me what happened, and you can go, okay? I know you didn't have anything to do with it. How could you? You were locked in a room."

"Sort of," Marco said.

This caught Christine's ear.

"You tell her," Toni said, turning away again. "It was your idea."

"Not completely," Marco protested, but it was apparent Toni wasn't going to say anything. So, he cleared his throat and said, "We wanted to elope."

Christine leaned back. That was the last thing she'd expected to hear. "Whoa. You're kidding. Your moms would have been furious!"

"*He* wanted to elope," Toni said, pointing at Marco. "I never had any intention of skipping out on my big day, not that I'll ever have one now."

"I'm sorry. I didn't mean to be insensitive. It caught me off guard."

"No worries. We're all having a bad day," Marco said before continuing. "You see, Mom and Val locked us in that room because they thought we were going to call off the wedding, but we were only goofing around. The thing is, getting locked in there wasn't funny, and I got pissed off. That's when we had an actual argument."

"I see," Christine said, taking more notes.

"I was pacing around the room, and I stepped on something that sounded hollow. When I moved the rug out of the way, I found a trap door—not that it was very well-hidden or anything. At first, we both went down, but then, we decided—"

"*You* decided," Toni interjected, folding her arms defiantly.

"*I* decided to play a prank on everyone that would get our mothers in a tizzy."

Christine stopped writing. "What was that, exactly?"

"Not kill Uncle Abe if that's what you're suggesting," Toni said.

"I'm not suggesting anything."

Marco waited to see if Toni was going to continue the story. When she didn't, he said, "Truth be told, I didn't know what I was going to do."

"That's when he came up with that hare-brained plan to pretend we'd killed each other," Toni said.

"It worked, didn't it?" Marco asked. "They bought it hook, line, and sinker, charging up there to break down the door. By that time, we weren't even there."

"Hold on," Christine said. "I know how hard this is, but please finish your story, Marco."

"Do you? Do you know how hard it is to find out your fiancée is related to you?" Toni snapped.

This brought the conversation to a screeching halt, and the three of them sat there in silence for a while. Not even the rain had the ability to defy the tower's sound-deadening properties, but the rumbling of thunder could be felt through the stones.

"Marco?" Christine whispered.

Jimi's son jumped at the sound of her voice. "Yeah?"

"Would you please finish the story?"

"Yeah, right. Okay. It turned out that the passage out of the Wallpaper Room led to the pulpit where Uncle Abe left his things. I almost took his Bible, but then I saw our marriage license and got the idea to elope. I didn't make it back to the room, though. I got about halfway up the tunnel when I met Toni, who'd decided to follow me. We snuck out of the castle and continued our discussion by the wishing well. That's where we decided—"

"*I* decided," Toni interjected. "I wasn't going to be one of those people who rushed into something and tossed their ring away."

Marco looked like he'd been punched. There was no doubt about it. *We* didn't exist anymore.

"I'm sorry. I don't follow," Christine said. "What ring?"

"While we were arguing, we noticed someone had thrown a wedding band into the wishing well," Marco explained. "I wanted to get it out in case they'd lost it by mistake, but Toni said I should leave it. She thought the person must have put it there for a good reason. Why else would they have thrown it in the well?"

"Oh."

"Anyway, after that, Toni said we needed to go through with the ceremony. So we rang the bell, and you know the rest."

"We didn't kill him," Toni stated emphatically. "We didn't know about all this until the same time you did."

Their story was so outlandish, Christine thought it had to be true. "I believe you, but who did? This whole thing has my mind tied in knots."

"Have you talked to everyone already?" Marco asked.

"Not quite. I still need to chat with Eddo."

"Eddo? Kill Abe? Not a chance. He's been my best friend since kindergarten."

"I know, but still, I have to talk to him. Not only that, but I'm getting tired of being up here. Let's go back down. I can talk to him in a corner or something."

As they descended the stairs, Christine called to Maisey, Bianca, and Tommy. They joined their small group, but no one said a word until they arrived at the great hall.

18. Dropping Like Flies

Like most people, Jimi relied on his phone to know what time it was. He'd tried wearing a smartwatch—the idea of it being strapped to his wrist was appealing to someone in his line of work—but it had gotten waterlogged and smashed on his first day at sea, so he hadn't bothered with anything like that again. Of course, that was neither here nor there, seeing as Gretta had safely confiscated everyone's electronic devices. And since rainclouds entirely blocked out the sky, he had no way of determining the time.

However, he was Jimi: meaning he had a sixth sense about these things, and he knew that night was waning fast. Soon, the sun would rise (whether they saw it or not), but what the day would bring was anyone's guess.

On the far side of the great hall, Christine appeared out of the velvet curtains. Flashes of lightning made her gentle features look sharp as Jimi watched her enter the space for the second time that night. He could tell she hadn't figured out who'd killed Abe yet, but he looked at her expectantly anyway.

Christine shook her head.

It wasn't the response he'd hoped to see.

Everyone except Val had been awake all night, and they looked more than a little worse for wear. Thoroughly talked out, the castle had become eerily silent, which was why people jumped out of their skin when Christine spoke.

"Has anyone seen Eddo?" she asked, wearily popping the top on a can of soda. "He's the last person I need to speak to. If nothing comes of that, we'll simply have to wait for the authorities to arrive in the morning."

Val jerked awake. "He said he needed a smoke, so he went to look for a place that wouldn't set off the detectors. He'll be back in a minute or two."

"When exactly was that?" Christine asked.

Val shook her head. She didn't know, having dozed off.

Opening a candy bar he'd bought from the vending machine, Marco asked, "Does anyone know when Gretta is supposed to open the doors? I need some real food. A Fisherman's Breakfast down at Zak's Place would do nicely."

Everyone's stomachs growled at the mention of a hearty Popplestone breakfast.

Frankie scrunched her face, trying to remember if Gretta had mentioned when she'd be back. "I wish I knew. I didn't think to ask. I never thought we'd be here all night. I figured we'd eat, have a couple of hours of fun searching the castle, and go home."

Marco tossed the wrapper in a trash can. "Some fun."

Tommy slapped his forehead. "I totally forgot about the escape room!"

Bianca gasped, realizing that she, too, had forgotten about the game. "Maybe we should do it to help pass the time. I know I'm not going to sleep tonight."

The hall was instantly filled with groans echoing off the stone walls like mournful ghosts. The sound went right up Val's spine, and she shivered.

Frankie was the only person who thought it was a good idea, and what the oldest Bellagamba sister wanted, she got. "Where's that paper with the clue?"

No one moved to find it.

"Well?"

"It's over there," Rose said, waving her hand dismissively.

Frankie rifled through the empties and found it stuck to the side of a can. She read it aloud.

> *On corners sharp and dungeons deep,*
> *where sun shines bright and shadows creep,*
> *I lurk amongst the wind-swept stones,*
> *or crawl beneath the castle's bones.*
>
> *Atop my perch, I've seen it all,*
> *from awe-struck lovers to somber pall*
> *walk my way, my vigil kept,*
> *a silent watch, as secrets slept.*
>
> *For in those places, you will see,*
> *many brethren of my breed,*
> *watching and waiting for you to pass,*
> *with stony eyes and ancient need.*
>
> *My charge protected, from tower high,*
> *Stone and earth and moon and sky,*
> *watching and waiting for you to pass,*
> *with stony hearts that never sigh.*
>
> *Follow my gaze to the bottom deep,*
> *where water glimmers and whispers sleep,*
> *A clue awaits all those who dare,*
> *to join in my eternal stare.*

"What in the world does that gobbledygook mean?" Rose asked, nearly falling out of her chair when she craned to look at the poem.

With something else to think about, Bianca looked happier than she had in hours. "I think it's kind of fun."

"Bad, you mean," Tommy said, wrinkling his nose. "Who wrote that anyway?"

"Probably Gretta," Maisey whispered.

He instantly clammed up. "Oh, yeah. Right."

Bianca took the clue from Frankie. "But what is it trying to tell us?"

"I've only seen water in one place, so we should start there," Jimi suggested.

"Right. I bet it has something to do with that creepy gargoyle fountain that fills the pool. Stoney eyes and all," Maisey suggested.

A loud scraping sound followed by a thump drew everyone's attention to the arch that led into the cloister. Above it, a stone had moved to the side, and a large hourglass had pushed out of the darkness behind. It was now in the process of turning over.

"But how?" Christine asked.

Frankie didn't care how the timer knew to start. Only that it had. "The game is timed?"

Jimi scratched his head. "It appears so."

"The question is, what happens if we don't solve the clues in time?" Tommy asked, taking Bianca's hand.

Frankie headed straight to the cloister. "I have no intention of finding out. It's just one more thing Abe didn't tell us. Let's go."

"I'll stay here with Toni. Tell us when you've figured it out," Val offered, but Frankie would have none of it.

"Oh, no. Until the doors open, we're sticking together, which means you're both coming with us."

"Whatever, big sis. You're the boss."

Still in a daze, Toni let Val lead her up the stairs, with Marco following sullenly behind. When they got to the top, everyone else was already looking at the gargoyle above the pool.

Christine moved closer. "What else could the clue be referencing other than that thing?"

"But how will we follow its gaze?" Maisey asked. "It sticks out from the wall over the water."

Past the storefronts and beyond the pool, there was another staircase to the second floor—the same one everyone had rushed up to check on Marco and Toni—but it was too narrow to fit everyone.

"I guess a few of us should go up the stairs and lean out of the arches," Tommy said, leading the way. "I've heard the people who built this place used to jump out of them into the pool.

"It's worth a shot," Jimi said, sitting on what he thought was a bench. "We can't see anything from down here."

"I couldn't even if I wanted to," Rose said, squinting at the water.

Bianca tapped Jimi on the shoulder. "Careful. That's some kind of little kid coffin."

Jimi looked down to see a blank, stony face looking up at him and quickly got up. "Let it never be said that this place isn't creepy."

"Uh-huh," the bridesmaid agreed.

"Come on," Tommy called to his friends. "That is super cool!"

Bianca squeezed next to him and grabbed the gargoyle's head to steady herself.

"Can you see it?" he asked, pointing at the water.

To everyone down below, the pool looked like a black mirror, making it impossible to see beneath the surface.

"Well, are you going to tell us?" Frankie asked.

"Oh yeah. It's a—"

"Ow!" Bianca screamed. "It bit me! It bit me!"

Freaked out by the sight of blood dripping from the gargoyle's teeth, Tommy pulled himself out of the window.

Maisey grabbed Bianca and pulled her back, too. "Christine, we need you!"

The nurse was up the stairs like a shot, passing a rather green Tommy as he slowly made his way in the other direction.

"Put pressure on that," Christine said before peeking her head through the nearest arch. "We're going to Bianca's room so she can have a lie-down. I'll clean and dress the cut up there. Jimi, you might want to take a look at that gargoyle. It's pretty strange."

"Why would they do that?" Bianca asked.

Christine was puzzled. "Do what?"

The bridesmaid pointed out the window.

It was impossible for the nurse to miss what she meant. The stone gargoyle had two sharp stainless steel teeth sticking straight up from its lower jaw, one of which was currently dripping with Bianca's blood. "I wouldn't read too much into it. By all accounts, the people who built this castle were pretty eccentric. They were probably trying to make the fountain look as menacing as possible." But she didn't believe it. It had been a strange and trying night—one Christine would very much like to put behind her, but would that ever be possible? More than likely, this night would haunt everyone in attendance the rest of their lives.

"Is she okay?" Jimi asked, climbing the stairs.

"She'll be fine. I'll be back in a few minutes after I get her squared away," Christine said, leading Bianca to the second floor.

"James Amato, are you going to tell us what the clue is or not?" an exasperated Frankie called up to him.

Jimi stuck his head out of the window and looked into the water. "Would you look at that? You can see it as clear as day from up here."

"And?"

"It's a cannon in the tiles. I mean, there's a rectangle with a cannon in it. Does that mean anything to anyone?"

"AHH!" Toni yelled, leaping up. She'd just realized she'd been sitting on the same sarcophagus Jimi had sat down on.

Frightened by the outburst, Rose slipped on the steps to the cloister.

"Jimi!" Frankie yelled. "Get down here!"

"Sorry, Maisey," he said. "Will you be okay?"

She was sitting on a step, staring into space. "Yeah. Just a bit shaken."

"Aren't we all? Got to go help Rose."

"Should I get Christine?"

"Nah, let's not bother her until we know what's going on. I don't know if anyone mentioned this to you, but Rose has a flair for the dramatic."

"You don't say?" Maisey asked.

The pair laughed, and Jimi scooted down the steps.

Marco and Frankie were already helping...or trying to help Rose...but she'd have none of it.

"Where's Jimi?" she wailed, waving her hands in the air.

"I'm right here, Rose. Tell me what happened."

"There was this terrible scream, and I fell down the steps."

"Let me see."

Rose lifted her dress higher than necessary to display her ankle.

Jimi pulled her dress back down. "It's just sprained. Let me help you to a chair."

"No! I mean, no, thank you. Please, take me to my room."

"Give me a break," Frankie said. "You are such a diva."

Jimi put an arm around Rose's waist and helped her up. "It's okay. I don't mind."

"You really have a winner here, Frankie. If I could be so lucky," Rose said, leaning her head on Jimi's shoulder.

Frankie scoffed. "If only."

"Come on, Mrs. Bellagamba," Maisey said, having followed Jimi down the stairs. "Let's get this over with."

Val lumbered ahead of what was left of their group. "Yeah, sis, let's go. You're the one who made us play this game in the first place. This way, everyone."

Tommy pointed after her. "Where's she going?"

"To the Command Center, I imagine," Frankie explained. "There's a cannon in there. We used to play in that room when we were kids."

Val led everyone past the formal dining room and kitchen, then down a short set of steps into a circular room adorned with a mural depicting the Revolutionary War *Battle of Popplestone Harbor.*

The pictorial was painted from the perspective of Ledge Island in the middle of the harbor. To the south, warships entered the port under full sail, firing their cannons. To the west, the town returned fire from both harbor-side forts, one on the western shore and one at the mouth of the Inner Harbor. To the north, buildings were set on fire as a landing party attempted to burn the town. And to the east, townsfolk lined the shore, firing on the interlopers, pinning them behind a grounded schooner. The focal point, however, was an oversized depiction of Sandy Bar Lighthouse, dispelling the darkness before dawn—an ever-present symbol of hope for the people of Popplestone who primarily made their living on the sea. But that wasn't everything in the room. Blueprints of weapons of war covered drafting tables, and the base of the walls were lined with all manner of ship paraphernalia, including eyepieces, brass bullseye windows, and an enormous capstan wrapped with a heavy rope.

And there, atop a wooden pedestal in the center of the room, sat one of Magnolia Castle's prized possessions: an antique brass signal cannon.

"It's a little small to defend the castle, don't you think?" Maisey asked facetiously.

"It's for signaling distress or announcing arrivals and things like that," Marco explained. "Not shooting other ships."

"As if I don't know that. I grew up in Popplestone, remember?"

"Yeah, sorry."

Frankie leaned close to read the plaque. "It says, *Recovered from the* Conquest, *1823.*"

With a stomach-turning bang, the two doors—the one that led back the way they came and the second that led to the next floor—slammed shut.

Everyone pounded on them with all their might and called for help, but no one came.

"They can't hear us," Marco said, leaning against the door. "It must be soundproof like the tower."

"What was their obsession with making things soundproof around here?" Tommy asked.

"From what I've seen," Maisey said, "I think the people who built this place enjoyed toying with their guests."

"No doubt."

The tension in the room reached a breaking point, and Frankie kicked the door with her foot.

Val pulled her sister back. "Keep calm, everyone. I'm sure this is part of the game."

Frankie wrenched her arm from Val's grasp. "Keep calm? That's funny coming from you!"

"At least I'm trying."

"Okay, what do we do? Shoot off the cannon?" Tommy asked, picking up the carved wooden mallet sitting next to it.

"Inside the castle?" Maisey grabbed it from him. "That's a stupid idea."

"I don't see you coming up with any suggestions." He grabbed the mallet back, but overextended and lost his footing. As if in slow motion, he fell toward the cannon, and everyone dove for cover.

BOOM!

When the mallet struck the firing pin, the half-charge blank that the castle typically used for events went off. Someone, probably Chuck, had forgotten to remove it after the day's festivities, as firing off a cannon sounded like a terrible idea to Gretta after everything that had happened.

Moaning in pain, Frankie, Val, Maisey, Tommy, Toni, and Marco slowly sat up or got to their feet. They'd all managed to protect their ears except Tommy, who was stumbling around the room, yelling, "Can anybody hear me? I think I lost my voice."

"You stupid boy!" Frankie said, wagging her finger at him, not that he heard her. "You could have killed someone."

"He did! I've been shot. I'm dead! Oh, I'm dead," Val wailed, collapsed on the floor. She clutched her left breast with one hand and groped in the air for the handle to the pearly gates. "I'm coming, Jesus! The Lord is calling me home. I love you, Toni! Be good. I'll be watching you from Heav—!"

WHACK!

Val stopped mid-wail. Frankie had slapped her across the face, but the shock had prevented the nerve endings from communicating with her brain, and she hadn't felt the pain yet.

"Get a hold of yourself. It was a blank," Frankie said. "You're not dead. You're just an idiot."

"AHH-OH-OW!" Val screamed when the pain finally registered. "You hit me! What if I were having a heart attack? What would you have thought then? I bet you'd be mad at yourself for being so callous!"

"Try me."

Marco looked aghast. "Mom!"

"Mrs. Bellagamba, really!" Maisey exclaimed, helping Val sit up. "Show a little compassion. That was pretty scary."

"If you're so worried about her, why don't you take her to her room? Take Tommy, too, while you're at it. I want him out of my sight!"

"I can't. The doors are—"

"Open," Marco said, pointing to the hallway.

"At least something good came of it," Frankie said, helping Maisey lift Val off the ground. "And...uh...I'm sorry, sis. Been a hard day."

"That's the understatement of the century," Marco added. "I'll help Maisey."

"She's got it. We need you here. There's still a clue to figure out. Don't you remember? We're on the clock."

The look on everyone's faces—except Tommy's, who hadn't heard a word of what Frankie said—showed they'd completely forgotten about the hourglass.

"How much time do we have?" Maisey asked.

Toni wiped a tear away from her eye. "I don't want to find out what happens if we don't finish before the sand runs out."

"Considering how the rest of this night has gone, I don't want to find out either," Frankie said, crossing her arms. "We're going to finish the game and get out of here."

Once Maisey, Val, and a shell-shocked Tommy left the room, the remaining team of Toni, Marco, and Frankie got down to business solving the clue. Or, more accurately, Marco and Frankie worked on it, and Toni stood in the corner sobbing.

"Talk to her, son," Frankie suggested.

"She doesn't want me anywhere near her, Mom. Can you blame her?"

"No, not really. Hey!"

"What is it?" Toni asked, turning around.

"There's a tiny inscription. What does it say, Marco? My eyes aren't what they used to be."

"Praise him with the timbrel and dance: praise him with stringed instruments and *pipes*. [Psalm 150:4] And the word pipes is italicized."

"That's not very dungeony," Toni said, struggling to fit her queenly dress into a chair.

"Sure it is," Frankie said. "There's a pulpit and pews and…"

"An organ!" all three said at the same time.

19. And Then There Was One

Back in the castle's great hall, Toni, Marco, and Frankie stared at the massive organ tucked into the corner.

"I hope we don't have to play it," Marco said. "My piano lessons never included feet."

Frankie shook her head. "I doubt it. There's a sign right there that says not to touch it."

Toni started whimpering again. "Then how do we figure out the clue?"

"What clue? I don't see—" Frankie stopped talking. "Oh, the lyrics."

All three squinted to see the words printed on the score.

> My eyes look out at the world, but I cannot see.
> I reflect my surroundings, but I am not a mirror.
> I can be small enough to fit in your pocket
> or big enough to cover a wall.
> What am I?

"That's a lousy song," Marco said, putting his hands on his hips. "It doesn't even rhyme."

Toni pursed her lips. "That's because it isn't a song, it's a riddle."

"More eyes," Frankie mumbled.

"What's that, Aunt Frankie?"

"My eyes look out at the world but cannot see," she said. "Hmm. My sisters and I used to have a riddle book, but I don't remember this one."

"It could be a statue like the gargoyle again," Marco suggested.

Frankie shook her head. "I doubt it. What would be the point of having two clues point to the same thing?"

"I reflect my surroundings, but I'm not a mirror. That's definitely not the gargoyle, but it could be the ocean," Toni said, walking toward the indoor part of the patio.

"What's small enough to fit in your pocket but big enough to cover a wall?" Marco asked. "Wallpaper? Paint?"

Toni scoffed at the suggestion. "Why would you carry paint in your pocket?"

"A swatch, maybe?"

"A-ha!" Frankie exclaimed. "I know what it is. A photograph."

"Great, Mom, but I haven't seen any photos. Just tapestries and paintings, and those," he said, pointing to the parallel rows of colorful banners hanging from the ceiling.

"Which means it should be pretty easy to find, but I'm going to leave that to the two of you. Jimi should have been back by now. I'm going to see what...or who...is keeping him."

"No way!" Toni said, backing away.

"Come on, Toni. Is it really that bad to be around me?" Marco asked.

She didn't answer.

Marco threw his hands in the air. "Fine. I'll do it myself."

Giving in, Toni made an exasperated noise and followed her ex-fiancée. "You'd better hurry up," she said, glancing at the hourglass. "I don't think there's much time left."

"Then get over here and help."

Minutes later, they found themselves standing in the center of the bridal room, looking at each other.

"You brought us here on purpose!" Toni yelled, stamping her foot on the ground.

"No, really. I didn't. It's the last room on this floor. We had to check it."

"Hmph."

"Listen, Toni, can we talk?"

"We don't have time for that. And besides, there's nothing to talk about. Not ever."

"Can't we still be friends?"

"No. I mean, not in that way."

"Of course not. That's not what I meant," Marco said, leaning against the wall. "You're my best friend."

Toni got a strange expression on her face.

"Am I that grotesque to you now?" he asked, but she wasn't looking at him.

"I found it!"

Hanging on the wall was the photograph they'd taken of the bridal party.

"That's got to be the final clue," she said. "Take it down, and check to see if there's anything on the back."

When Marco pulled on the frame, a small wire attached to it popped off. Suddenly, the great hall was filled with the sound of bells and trumpets.

"What's going on?" the others called down, descending the stairs into the hall.

"We figured it out!" Toni said, waving the photo over her head as she ran from the bridal room.

"Hey, what's that?" Tommy asked, bringing up the rear. "Is that a telephone ringing?"

"Clear away the empties," Jimi instructed. "And put the photo on the table so we can all see it."

On the back, they found a message written in a fine script.

Congratulations!
You have disarmed the trap and foiled Count Mountebane's dastardly plan. Now, complete your quest by sounding the all clear.

"Did Father Abraham tell anyone how to do that?" Maisey asked.

Christine put an arm around the matron of honor, "Don't worry. We've gotten this far. We'll figure it out."

Jimi turned the photo over, and they leaned in.

"That's a pretty good picture," Tommy said, standing on his tiptoes to see. "Where did you get it?"

"Just a second. Can I see that?" Christine asked, taking the picture. "I don't believe it."

Frankie grabbed it from her. "What? What do you see?"

"It's not what I see. It's what I *don't* see. Someone's missing."

"Yeah, right. Eddo," Tommy said, his hearing slowly returning. "I gave him the pen and stuff. He said he had to bring it to Father Abraham, but must not have gotten back in time for the photo."

"The inkwell?" Frankie asked.

"Yeah."

"But Father Abraham's standing right there," Christine said, pointing to the photograph. "That's when it must have happened."

Jimi knitted his brow. "What happened?"

"No idea, but remember what I smelled on Father Abraham's hands? Think Christine. Right. In the *Cranberry Spritzer Murder*, Ms. Langenshire explained that *cyanide kills quickly if you drink it, but it takes longer if you get it on your skin*. That's why Father Abraham got sick. It took time for the poison to take effect."

"Are you saying Eddo poisoned my brother? But why?"

"I don't know, but we have to find him. Didn't you say he went for a smoke? Well, by now, he could have finished the whole pack!"

"Then where did he go?" Maisey asked. "We can't leave, and we've been all over the castle."

"Ahhhh!" Toni screamed. She was staring through the patio window.

There, standing in the pouring rain like a living gargoyle, was a solitary figure high atop the castle's tower.

20. *Angel Wings*

After a heated discussion on who should go, Jimi and Christine climbed the tower's spiral stone stairs toward the roof. Jimi had wanted to go alone, but no one thought that was a good idea. If Eddo really was the murderer, the situation might get out of control quickly.

In an unusual display of affection, Frankie had kissed Jimi and hugged him. "Be careful, you big lug."

"I've been caught in hurricanes, fires, and a waterspout, and you've never worried about me before."

"Because you know the ocean. This is different."

Jimi hugged her back. "Yeah. I know."

When he turned to leave, Rose grabbed him and kissed him square on the lips. "Don't go! Frankie needs you. I need you!"

"You need me?" Jimi asked, wiping the lipstick off his mouth.

Frankie and Val grabbed their youngest sister by the arms and pulled her back.

"You're spell won't work on him," Frankie said. "Jimi'd never leave me."

"How do you know?" Rose asked.

"Because he loves me, warts and all."

"That, I do. You're my rock," he said and headed for the tower.

"Not without me," Christine called after him.

"I still can't wrap my head around it," Popplestone's weathered harbormaster said, as they spiraled their way toward the chapel. "It doesn't make any sense."

Christine followed closely behind. "Ms. L. says there's always a reason. You just have to find it."

When they reached the metal ladder leading to the roof, they climbed the final few feet and opened the hatch, only to be blasted by pelting rain.

"You stay here," Jimi yelled over the shrieking wind.

"No chance. I'm coming with you."

"Christine, there's no reason for us both to risk our lives. Stay on the ladder. If I need you, I'll call for you."

"Okay, but if I don't like the look of things, I'm coming out."

Jimi nodded and pulled himself onto the roof.

Eddo was about ten feet away. He had one leg over the side, staring into the abyss that was the Atlantic Ocean during a storm. Jimi had seen that look in many a sailor's eye, and it rarely spoke of more than defeat, which meant Marco's best man probably thought he had nothing left to lose.

Risking a glance over the side, Jimi quickly pulled back. He'd seen what a storm on the sea could do up close and personal, but viewing it from on top of an unprotected castle tower lent an entirely new level of danger he hadn't anticipated. As quickly as possible, he knelt to prevent himself from being blown off.

"Hey, Eddo," he said, raising his voice loud enough to be heard but not yelling.

Far below, many terrified faces peered out the patio window, staring up at them.

"Jimi," Eddo replied, not turning around.

"Why don't you come inside where we can talk?"

"Nah. Here's good."

"But you're soaked to the bone. You must be freezing."

"Can't really feel it," Eddo said, staring at the white-crested black water roiling beneath them.

Jimi felt strange trying to keep the conversation going. Usually, that's what people did to him. "Can you tell me what happened?"

"You know."

"No, I don't. If you'd just—"

"Don't lie to me!" Eddo snapped.

Jimi flinched. He needed to be careful. Taking a moment to collect his thoughts, he thought about how this was usually his favorite time of day, just before dawn. Any other morning, he'd be at the *DnD,* buying a coffee—black, no sugar—from Dottie or Danielle. Honestly, he preferred Dottie because she always winked at him and threw in a cruller. Then, he'd chat with some of his buddies for a minute or two and stop by the office to check his messages before heading to the docks to crank up the engine and make his rounds, but not today.

Hoping Eddo had calmed down, he said, "I'm not lying. We don't know what happened. That's why Christine and I came up here. We were hoping you'd tell us."

For the first time, Eddo turned toward him, making his position even more precarious.

"I promise. No funny business," Jimi said, showing Eddo his hands and leaning against the faux battlement wall.

As if on cue, the rain worsened, and Jimi slid a little closer so he could hear what his son's former best man had to say.

Eddo put his other leg over the edge, and Jimi moved to grab him but stopped. Eddo wasn't going over the edge. At least, not yet.

"Who knew things would end this way?" Eddo said, sounding more matter-of-fact than nostalgic. "I imagine my Dad is wondering where I am. I guess he'll be pullin' the pots without me."

"No one is going out today. Not in this. And nothing is ending."

"Really? That's what you think? Because I'm seein' it a different way."

Jimi leaned his head back on the hard, wet stone. Eddo was right. Nothing would be the same after what had happened.

The young man hung his head. "If only I hadn't seen that birthmark."

The cold rain and flashes of lightning had a way of interrupting a person's train of thought, and Jimi struggled to understand what Eddo meant. "What birthmark? Toni's butterfly?"

"Angel wings. They're angel wings."

"Oh. I didn't know that. I'd always been told it was a butterfly."

"I knew she had it," Eddo said, "but I didn't put two and two together until I saw it. Growing up, she covered it with long-sleeved bathing suits and stuff."

That was true. Toni had hidden her birthmark for years, not out of vanity or embarrassment but because she planned to reveal it on her wedding day. And reveal it she had.

That felt like a lifetime ago to Jimi. "Does this have to do with what Toni's grandmother wrote in that note?"

"My grandmother, you mean."

"Did she know Toni?"

"No, you don't get it. I'm Toni's twin brother."

Jimi reflexively laughed, but when he saw the drawn look on Eddo's face, he realized the young man was speaking the truth. "I'm afraid I don't understand."

"It's not that hard to get," Eddo explained, leaning farther over the edge and looking toward the ground. "You know I'm adopted, right?"

"Yes. So's Toni. Lots of people are."

"Well, when my mom—Rose, I guess—put me up for adoption, my grandmother gave my new parents a gift. This." Eddo pulled a chain from under his shirt. At the end was a St. Philomena medal. "I've always worn it."

"Yes, I remember it. Lots of newborns are given pendants like that. She's the patron saint of babies."

"It's not a pendant. It's a locket," Eddo said, displaying it on the palm of his hand.

Jimi saw where this was going, and he grew uncomfortable. He didn't know how to ask, but he needed to see what was inside. Luckily, he didn't have to. Shielding its contents from the rain, Eddo popped it open and handed it to him.

"Are you sure?" Jimi asked.

Eddo nodded.

Inside, there was a tiny note.

> *For my beautiful grandson. You are loved. You have a sister. Find her someday. She has a birthmark in the shape of angel wings on her right arm.*
>
> *Love always,*
> *Nonna*

Jimi's mouth dropped open. "It's true. You're—"

"Toni's brother. And, as it turns out, Marco's half-brother. Apparently, *Father* was an apt title for Abraham, don't you think? He certainly got around for a priest."

"But it all happened before he took the cloth," Jimi said without considering what he was suggesting.

"Oh, it's okay then."

"Sorry. That didn't come out right."

"It's true, though. Sins are forgiven and all," Eddo said, taking the pendant back and putting it around his neck.

Jimi didn't like the direction the conversation was taking, so he tried to encourage Eddo to keep telling his story. "When did you figure that out?"

"Actually, it was something you said."

"Me? But I didn't know."

"After carrying Rose's bags into the lobby, I walked to the water to finish my smoke. That's when I overheard you and Father Abraham—Dad, I guess—talking. You said, *I've always thought Marco was more like you than me*, and it clicked."

"You mean, you realized you were related?"

"Yeah, sort of. Toni had shown me her dress earlier in the day. She wasn't into hiding like most brides, too excited about finally showing off her birthmark, I guess. That threw me for a loop."

"I bet. What did you do?"

"I stood there looking at you and Father Abraham, and I saw the similarities. Too many similarities. The darker red hair, the shape of my ears. Toni's ears. Father Abraham's ears. Then, I thought about how people used to confuse us in school when we were kids. I told myself, *You could be Marco's brother, you look so much alike*, and it hit me. The three of us had to be related."

The more Jimi considered this, the more he couldn't believe he'd never seen it before.

"I got angry," Eddo continued, "like I was going to explode. I don't know why, but I screamed that it was Marco's fault, and the whole place erupted. I didn't mean for that to happen, but I loved it. Everyone was fighting. It felt good. It looked like how I felt inside. Then I got dark. Really dark. I had tunnel vision. I tried to walk it off, but I couldn't. I wound up sitting in the old workshop under the castle."

Jimi listened, stunned by what Eddo was saying.

"I was mad at him. Your brother, I mean. How could he do that? He gave us away, but we still grew up together. How screwed up is that? And we didn't know!"

"Pretty messed up," Jimi agreed. "But why didn't you say anything?"

"I was Marco's best man. I couldn't do that to him on his wedding day."

"But you'd figured out that he and Toni were half-siblings. You must have known they couldn't get married."

"Yeah, but I wasn't thinking clearly."

"What happened after that?"

"I found an old box of rat poison in the workshop, and I had the idea to put it in the ink."

"Wait. You poisoned the ink?"

"Yeah. I broke the pen, too, so Abraham would get it on his hands. I figured it was stupid and probably wouldn't work, but I did it anyway. Then it *did* work. I mean, it totally killed him, and I was locked in the castle with his dead body and all of you. I didn't know what to do, so I kept my distance as much as I could and came here."

A bolt of lightning shot across the sky, followed by a thunderous crash that nearly knocked Jimi off the roof. "That was close! We have to get off the roof."

Eddo got up and stood with his arms out. "Maybe I should let the lightning strike me down for my sins. The *Hand of God* and all."

"Don't talk that way. I'm not saying it's going to be easy, but we'll get through it. You're family now, and family sticks together."

Seeing the distress on Jimi's face, Eddo put his arms down. "You know I wasn't going to jump, right? I just needed some air."

But at that instant, a crack of lightning so loud the tower shook exploded from the sky, and Eddo slipped on the wet stones.

"No!" Jimi yelled as Eddo went over the side. Without regard for his own safety, Jimi threw himself toward the edge and grabbed Eddo's hand in the nick of time. "I've got you, buddy, and I'm never letting go."

At the sound of Jimi yelling, Christine had climbed to the roof and was now holding onto his feet.

There they were, lying on the roof, holding onto each other with Eddo dangling by one hand.

"Give me your other hand," Jimi yelled as the storm intensified.

But Eddo wasn't looking at him. He was staring out over the water with a faraway look in his eyes.

"Right now, buddy. Just swing your other hand to me. Quickly now. I'm losing my grip."

Eddo slowly raised his eyes to Popplestone's indefatigable harbormaster and said, "You know, I always wanted a sister."

Then, his wet hand slipped out of Jimi's, and he fell.

• • • • •

"You're still here?" Gretta asked, rubbing her eyes. She was wearing pink footie pajamas, her hair was a mess, and she had a set of heavy noise-cancelling headphones around her neck. "Why didn't Chuck close up after you finished the game?"

Flabbergasted at seeing her, Frankie asked, "Were you sleeping here the whole time?"

"Of course. You didn't think we'd let a drunk wedding party roam about the castle, did you? Chuck was supposed to keep an eye on you and when you finished the game, show you to the door."

"We never saw Chuck," Maisey said.

"That lazy…no good…son of a—"

"Gretta?" Frankie asked. "There's something we have to tell you."

"What?"

"We need to go outside. Will you let us out?"

"In this?"

"Yes."

"Well, go ahead if you need to. It's not like the doors are locked."

"Yes, they are," Val said. "We heard them lock."

"That was just part of the game. We couldn't lock you in. That would be against the law. Father Abraham knew that. Why didn't he say anything?"

A stunned silence fell over everyone as what Gretta said sank in.

Tommy, who was still speaking too loudly after the incident with the cannon, said, "She doesn't know."

"Know what?"

"You'd better sit down," Maisey said, leading Gretta to a chair.

"Why."

"Who's going to tell her?" Bianca asked, her voice wavering.

Frankie said, "I will."

By this time, Gretta realized something bad had happened. "Did you break something? I'll be in big trouble if you did. And where is Chuck?"

"Drunk in the basement for all we know," Rose said.

By now, Gretta was sitting in a chair surrounded by the bridal party.

Frankie looked directly at her and said, "Father Abraham is dead."

"That's not funny."

"It's not a joke."

"What? No. That can't be. The paramedics would have woken me."

"There were no paramedics. You had our phones and we were locked in, remember?"

"But you could have come to the office and gotten me. I can't hear anything with my headphones on. You see, I need the sound of the ocean to sleep."

"She's in shock, isn't she?" Bianca asked Tommy. "I wish Christine were here."

Frankie got in front of Gretta and pointed at the second floor. "He's up there."

"In Heaven?"

"No, in the guest bedroom."

"THERE'S A DEAD BODY IN THE CASTLE?"

At the same instant, Toni screamed, and everyone ran back to the patio windows. High above the ground, Jimi was hanging over the side of the tower, with Eddo dangling below him. Gretta pushed through, saw what was happening, and collapsed to the floor.

"Someone check her for a phone!" Frankie said, unable to look away from the terrifying sight unfolding atop the tower.

"Got it!" Maisey said, holding it up, but it was too late.

"Eddo!" Marco yelled, pressing his face hard against the glass. "Eddo..."

Epilogue

"There's my favorite nurse!" Maisey said, tiptoeing across the hot sand.

"Hey there. Come sit under my umbrella," Christine offered, putting her book down. "It's a scorcher today!"

"Thanks. I hoped I'd find someone. I hate going to the beach by myself."

"I hear you, but being alone with a good book can be nice, too."

"Oh, yeah? What are you reading?" Maisey asked, pulling out a beach towel and taking off her cover-up.

Christine looked at the cover. "Um…*The Unsolved Mystery of the Granite Quarry Murders*. It's about a killer in the '50s who dumped bodies in quarries all over the Cape Eider. No one ever found out who did it."

"Yikes! Really?"

"Yup."

"Are there bodies still down there? I mean, I go swimming at Iron Winch all the time."

Christine laughed. "No, there aren't any bodies in there anymore. At least, not that I know of. Not unless someone has put more in."

Maisey looked shocked and then realized Christine was pulling her leg. "Stop it!" she said, picking up the book and reading the description on the back cover. Returning it, she retrieved a clip from her bag to put up her hair. "I thought you liked fiction."

Christine took the book back. "I'm branching out. Where's Geoff? Doesn't he like the beach?

"He got called away on business. Work. Work. Work."

"I see."

"Say, did you hear about Bianca and Tommy?" Maisey asked.

"Sure did. I even got an invitation. But I can't believe they're going to get married at Magnolia Castle! Never in a million years did I think we'd go back there again."

"It's totally bizarre, which is probably why they're doing it."

"That sounds like them," Christine agreed, helping put suntan lotion on Maisey's back. "At least they won't have to worry about getting locked in."

"I know! I thought everyone was going to faint when Gretta said it was only a game and the doors were never locked."

"And that she was sleeping in the office!" Christine added. "We should have known they wouldn't leave us in the castle alone. How stupid were we?"

"Pretty stupid!" Maisey said, stopping herself just in time. She was about to throw her hands in the air, but remembered she was holding the strings to her bikini. "Whoops. Almost gave everyone a show," she said, tying her bathing suit back on when Christine finished. "None of us even tried the doors or thought about getting our phones from the office!"

"Power of suggestion, I guess."

"I guess."

Christine sat quietly watching the water lap the shore. If there was ever a right place to reflect, it was the beach. To her right, children floated down the river that flowed from the marsh to the sea.

She turned to Maisey. "I still can't believe Eddo survived the fall."

"And didn't get skewered on one of the tent poles."

"True. He was lucky to escape with only broken bones. It could have been much worse."

Maisey wrinkled her nose. "It was pretty awful anyway."

"In so many ways."

"I heard you aren't working at the hospital anymore. Is that true? Now you read stories to people, right?"

"Yes," Christine said slowly. "And I know what you're getting at."

"Well?"

"Yes, I visit the penitentiary. And yes, I've seen Eddo."

"No way," Maisey gasped. "That's weird!"

"Jimi's been by, too. I've heard Frankie, Val, and Rose have all put in requests to see him, but I don't think they'll be able to. They're under house arrest until the trial starts."

"Do you think they'll go to jail? I mean, he was already dead when they killed him."

"Who knows?"

Maisey brushed the sand off her toes. "If that had happened to me, I would have been out of my mind, too. The whole thing was nuts."

"Definitely."

"You know, I used to come here with Toni all the time. When we were ten, our parents would drop us off at the bridge, and we'd spend the whole day here."

"She'll be back. Many people visit the island, but few ever leave completely. Besides, Marco's here," Christine added, picking up her book.

"What?"

"I don't mean it that way, and you know it. Deep down, they love each other. In a different way, of course, but they still love each other. She'll want to see her brother and Val again. Toni just needs time."

"I guess you're right. I think I'll cool off. Want to come?"

Christine opened her book. "No thanks. The cops have discovered the second body in the quarry, and I'm about to find out who it is. I think it's the librarian!"

"How do you read that stuff after what happened?"

"I think I enjoy it more after the wedding."

"That's strange."

"I know," Christine said with a twinkle in her eye, and they both laughed.

Maisey trotted off. "You can sit there and bake. I'm going to see how cold the water is."

"You know the saying, *cold as a witch's*—"

"Christine! You're so naughty. And I thought you said you'd been reading."

"I dipped my feet."

"Scandalous! See you in a bit."

Maisey ran toward the water, but didn't make it far before seeing another sun soaker she knew.

"Take your time," Christine said, leaning back and closing her eyes. "Naps are good, too, especially on hot summer days. Murder will have to wait."

Ms. Prissy Langenshire's
GUIDE to FIGURING
Out if You've Been
MURDERED

Bradlie K. Roberts

CHAPTER 1

Mr. Marvin Baverstock of *Baverstock's Hay and Feed* died on Tuesday, August 7th, as predicted. His *Last Will and Testament* will be read at the offices of Hatchett, Aycock, & Haversham on West Wiley Street, and unless I am very much mistaken, it is unlikely to be well attended.

He is survived by his ex-wife, Matilda Baverstock, who is keeping the name because she hasn't found a suitable replacement yet. They have no children to speak of. That is to say, they did bear children—Mildred, Marjorie, and Waldo—but where those three are concerned, the less said, the better. Evidently, their parents' imagination was expended by the time they reached their third child. That, or they were holding the paper upside down.

An interesting fact is that neither Marvin nor Matilda had any prior farming experience when they opened their shop. However, seeing a need in the community, they moved into the Gramercy building after old Gramercy (not the original but of the third generation) sold it to the Baverstocks for a dollar. Truth be told, the warehouse was worth a lot more than that, but he'd had enough of coopering and, in a fit of rage, yelled, "The first person who gives me a dollar can have the lot!"

That person happened to be Martin—not because he wanted to purchase the building but because he'd retrieved a dollar from his wallet to pay for a pickle he'd fished out of the barrel by the front door. Old Gramercy snatched it from his hand, and Baverstock's Hay and Feed was born.

If only Mr. Baverstock had spoken to me sooner, I might have been able to direct him down a different path, but as it was, events had already been set in motion that would lead to his inevitable demise.

to be continued…

ABOUT THE AUTHOR

Bradlie K. Roberts loves her family more than any-thing in the world, never misses an opportunity to laze around with a good book, and can't get enough of decorating cookies and cupcakes for holidays and school events. She lives in a beautiful coastal town in New England with everything you'd expect: sandy beaches, rocky shores, a bustling downtown, and a mysterious castle.

251 CF